CROSSING THE TEES

THE **SIXTH** SHORT STORY ANTHOLOGY

6e

Published in paperback in 2023 by Sixth Element Publishing
on behalf of Crossing The Tees Book Festival

Sixth Element Publishing
Arthur Robinson House
13-14 The Green
Billingham TS23 1EU
www.6epublishing.net

ISBN 978-1-914170-39-3

British Library Cataloguing in Publication Data. A catalogue record for this book is available from the British Library.

Printed in Great Britain.

CONTENTS

FOREWORD

With the triumphant return of the Crossing the Tees Book Festival in June 2022, featuring a fantastic hybrid mix of in person and online events, the short story competition received another record number of entries.

Writers from around the world joined our Teesside-based writers to send in a fabulous array of stories. Shortlisting down to the thirty-one stories featured in this anthology was more difficult than ever, producing a wonderful collection and, as always, an entertaining, thought-provoking read.

Many thanks to the judges, author James Harris, author and bookseller Jenna Warren and former librarian Ian Wilson, who reported back that the competition had been a real pleasure to judge.

We'd like to thank everyone who entered the short story competition and wish you all happy writing for the coming year.

Gillie Hatton and Graeme Wilkinson

Sixth Element Publishing

2022-23

FIRST PLACE

CROSSING THE T'S
PHILIP SCULTHORPE

The actual form of dyslexia which I have is somewhat rare, in that it only expresses itself when I write.

I can read fluently but, the moment I set pen to paper, some kind of short-circuit happens in my brain, which makes me twist about all the rules of letter-forming. For years I systematically wrote my *e's* upside-down; used an *o* where an *a* should be (and vice versa); and routinely crossed my *i's* and dotted my *t's*.

My *i's* all looked like addition signs; every *t* wore a kind of umlaut.

After years of effort, I have eventually learned how to dot the *i's*, but I am, I know, unlikely to ever master crossing the *t's*.

To make matters worse, the spelling of words, which makes perfect sense to me when I read, becomes an arcane mystery when I write.

I regularly twist the rule of *i before e except after c*; can never work out why some plurals take an *ies* while others make do with only a single *s* by itself; and I can never ever divine where a possessive apostrophe should go.

It is a particularly disabling form of dyslexia since, as I say, it does not express itself when reading. So, I am able to read my own notes – I just don't have a clue what they say.

As well as the natural bond that exists between a father and his son, the fact that we both suffered from the same form of dyslexia made Father and I particularly close.

He had had little formal education, but was far from being a stupid man. He valued learning and, because of his magpie mind, there were few subjects upon which he could not discourse at length.

I take after him.

Perhaps our dyslexia made our brains form connections between ideas and statements that seemed bizarre to other people, but were perfectly sensible to us. Our conversations could range very far and very wide. Indeed, that was the joy of them.

In truth, Father was my only friend.

I was, after all, exactly the kind of child who was a natural target for bullies. At school I suffered the whole repertoire of name-calling, having my possessions stolen, and having to endure random acts of physical violence. Home – particularly Father's shed, filled by his comforting presence – was my sanctuary and the place I looked to for intellectual stimulation. I learned more from my father than ever I did from school.

I suppose I always knew in my heart that one day I would lose him, but I didn't suppose it would be quite so soon.

I suppose, too, I always knew, that once he was gone, life would become even more bleak and difficult – and so it proved.

What I didn't know is that our last conversation would resonate strangely through the years, hibernating somewhere at the back of my mind, only to suddenly awaken in the therapist's room this morning to resolve a long-standing misadventure.

That last time together, I was sat in Father's shed, watching him collect together the required tools for that day's activity. An inveterate modeller and DIY man, Father devised a project every Sunday for us to work on jointly.

Because he was a stickler for not beginning until he had the right equipment to hand, I knew I might be waiting for some time so, to kill a few moments, I took down a book from his shelves.

Father's bookshelves reflected his scattergun interests, so you never knew quite what a random selection might bring. Amongst the inevitable collection of joinery, decorating and home maintenance manuals acquired over the years, were volumes on such diverse subjects as ship's figureheads, Soviet brutalist architecture and the songbirds of Peru.

"What have you picked up there?" he asked.

"It's about something called synchronicity," I answered.

Father paused. He put down the wire cutters he'd been in the act of picking up, as if it were too challenging to select tools and consider philosophical issues simultaneously.

"It says here that Jung defined synchronicity as the occurrence of meaningful coincidences that actually have no cause."

"He did," said Father. "But I've always assumed Jung saw synchronicity as a subjective phenomenon, rather than a causal reality."

I took a moment to let the full import of what he'd said sink in. Then a thought struck me. "Could synchronicity be the reason you and I both always ask for toast at breakfast?"

"I thought we were going to build a radio together," said Father, removing *A Basic Introduction to Psychoanalytical Theory* from my hands.

He passed me a different volume and said, "I think you'll find the diagram we require is on page ninety-five."

I turned to page ninety-five, but found no diagram. Only a quotation, which I read out, 'Give me a child until he is seven and I will give you the man'.

"I thought I'd handed you *Practical Electronics for Boys*," said Father, somewhat vexed.

Obviously, he hadn't.

"Who said that?" I asked.

"The Jesuits, I believe. Give me that volume of quotations back. This won't get a radio built."

This time he more carefully selected a large encyclopaedic tome to replace it.

"Page ninety-five," he reminded me.

But this page ninety-five didn't contain a diagram either.

"Just another quotation," I said.

"Is it anything to do with sound waves?"

"I don't think so. It says, 'The child is father of the man'."

"Ah, William Wordsworth," murmured Father, "the great Lakeland poet."

"Was he a Jesuit?" I said.

"No, and that isn't *Practical Electronics for Boys* either. Have you been moving my books about?"

I hadn't.

"But is it evidence of synchronicity, do you think?" I asked.

"In what way?"

"Two random quotations, from two random books, essentially making the same point."

"A possibility," he said. "But thinking back to what you said earlier about toast, if you and I are governed by synchronicity then why do I like Marmite and you don't?"

That was a poser.

"You know," he added, glancing at his watch, "it's too late to start making a radio now. I might as well put these tools back."

Having said which – almost as if to underline that this truly was the end of the session – he suddenly clutched his chest, turned a horrible mottled blue colour, and slumped to the floor.

He had had a massive coronary and was dead within seconds.

That day he had been intending to show me how to wire a cat's whisker. As a consequence of not being able to find the right book (and of him deciding to die), it's a thing I am still unable to do.

But the question of how synchronicity operates in the world has never quite left my mind.

Later, I was interviewed by a man from the Coroner's Office who asked me what time the death occurred.

"Father would have said it was quarter past nine, but it was actually quarter to three."

The man from the Coroner's Office looked mystified.

"He always got the big hand and the little hand mixed up," I explained.

"Oh," the man from the Coroner's Office said.

"He suffered from a rare form of dyslexia. I take after him."

"So you have difficulty reading?"

"No. That's what's rare about it: the dyslexia only expresses itself when we start to write. My father could read perfectly. As I can."

"But not tell the time?"

"That's numbers isn't it? A totally different issue."

"But you can tell the time?"

"No, I have the same problem."

"How do you know it was quarter to three, then, not quarter past nine?"

"I held his watch up to the mirror."

The man from the Coroner's Office decided not to

pursue the question any further. He moved on to the next item on his form.

"What was your father doing when he became ill? Was he physically exerting himself?"

"He was explaining synchronicity to me."

"So his heart attack was likely just a random event?"

"I'm not sure," I said. "After all, if Jung's theory of synchronicity is correct, a second event may have occurred somewhere which, though not causative, still might seem meaningfully related."

The man from the Coroner's Office gave me the same look that my schoolteachers have given me all my life.

Teachers struggled to know how to deal with me.

I think one or two of them considered it possible I might be some form of idiot savant, who wrote in an amazingly complicated, uncrackable code of his own devising. Most of them, though, found it easier to simply treat me as a plain idiot, leaving me to languish at the back of the class.

They certainly didn't ever intervene to stop the incessant bullying.

Although there was one who – I suppose feeling pity after my father's demise – decided to reach out to me.

How odd then that it should be his act of kindness that initiated the blackest and most miserable period of my existence.

That probably shouldn't surprise you. I've already warned you, my life was to become much more bleak and difficult after Father's passing.

The day after the funeral, Mr Jenkins summoned me to his office.

"It's time we got you sorted out," he said, picking up the phone. "I'm going to call the Child Psychology Service."

I have very acute hearing and, either because of that, or because the person on the other end of the line had a voice like a water buffalo, once Mr Jenkins got through I heard every word.

"Is that Child Psychology?"

"Yes," came the reply.

"Can you see one of my pupils?"

"Of course not," said the voice on the other end, "we're on the telephone and I'm twenty-five miles from you."

"I didn't mean can you see them this very minute."

"That's good, because we've got a waiting list."

"How long before you could see him?"

"It depends on the problem. What is it?"

"I have a boy who crosses his *i's*."

"Crosses his eyes?"

"That's what I said: he crosses his *i's*."

"If he crosses his eyes, I honestly think an optician would be the most suitable referral."

"Oh, well you're the expert," said Mr Jenkins, putting the phone down and musing, *sotto voce*, as he did so, "What a loud voice that man had."

Even his *sotto voce* was not quiet enough for my sharp ears.

"I thought it sounded more like a woman."

"Crikey, if you can't tell the difference between a man and a woman, we definitely should get you to an optician."

Accordingly, I was sent to the one on the High Street, and he quickly determined I had perfect eyesight.

"Why have you been sent to me?" he asked.

"I cross my *i's*."

"Your *i's* or your eyes?"

"My *i's*."

"Ah, I see the problem. This is an example of Homophonic Inexactitude."

I nodded, though unsure what he meant. Despite my wide reading, it was a term I hadn't yet come across.

"A misunderstanding arising from two words, spelled differently, and with different meanings, but sounding the same to the ear," he clarified.

"Ah. You learned that at optician training school?"

"Only incidentally. At college I was President of the George Bernard Shaw Society, so became familiar with his opinions on the need to introduce clearer phonetic spelling to the English language."

I'd heard of George Bernard Shaw. My father often mentioned him. I assumed this chap must know what he was talking about. "Will glasses help?" I asked.

"No,' he said, "but I'll prescribe a pair anyway, or I won't get a fee. Just plain glass for you."

However, by one of those administrative confusions that can bedevil even the best regulated systems, I somehow ended up being issued spectacles that, in retrospect, I realise were meant for another.

Not knowing then that the spectacles should not have been mine, I put them on. They had lenses genuinely thick as milk bottle bottoms. Instantly, the world became only a vague blur of colour.

Suddenly I was unable to see the blackboard, or indeed, see anything clearly, and began regularly walking into walls and bumping into the furniture. Mr Jenkins felt deflated. His intervention appeared to have served only to make me develop acute dyspraxia.

Alas, we were not yet at the nadir of my life's journey.

'Bug' Simpson, the school's aged Head of Biology, was one of those teachers who held to the opinion that a tendency to clumsiness could best be dealt with by beating it out of a child.

However, annoyingly for him, corporal punishment with the cane had recently been banned at the school the previous year. Cleverly, he found a way round this restriction by chastising pupils with an old, but rather large, coffee tin.

Holding it by the lid, he would let the main body of the tin swing upon the hinge and deliver a stinging blow to the child in question.

It hurt fiercely, but if he was careful to land the flat of the metal upon you rather than an edge, then the mark it left soon dissipated, leaving little evidence of his brutality. For all that I despised him, I had to accept it was skilfully done.

His campaign of regular whacking continued relentlessly for some months. I remained just as clumsy.

I am probably one of the very few children to claim that being bullied can occasionally have positive outcomes.

One day, while pummelling me in the playground, one of my classmates smashed my spectacles. Suddenly, after so long, I could see properly again.

It was like a religious conversion.

My clumsiness departed as if it were a demon that had been exorcised. 'Bug' Simpson found no justification for continuing to hit me with his coffee tin. Soon after, he retired, a disappointed man.

Those spectacles became a comfort item for me. Glued together, I carried them in my pocket at all times and, when things got particularly bad, I would touch them to remind myself that even the darkest hour eventually has a dawn.

You might be thinking that this marked the beginning of happier times for me and, I suppose, life did improve a little. Not a lot, just a little.

You might also be wondering about my earlier statement, that my last conversation with my father somehow resolved a long-standing misadventure.

Let me elaborate.

While it is not in the same category as fighting in a war, or witnessing a horrifying event, I found having been regularly struck with a coffee tin led, later in life, to continuing low-level emotional problems. Even five years after leaving school, the smell of coffee brewing could still make me break out in a sweat.

I considered therapy but only recently did I pluck up courage enough to carry it through.

This morning was my initial appointment.

"Come in," said the therapist, "take a seat and tell me what the problem is."

"I think I may be suffering from post-traumatic stress disorder."

"How unfortunate," he said, sympathetically. "Before we talk, to help you relax, should I make you a nice cup of coffee?"

It was a good twenty minutes before my palpitations subsided.

The therapist waited patiently for me to calm myself before he spoke.

"I'll have to charge you for those twenty minutes, you know.'"

"But we haven't spoken yet."

"The session had begun though."

"But I was too breathless to talk."

"I was ready to listen."

The consultation failed to improve. I found him remote and difficult to engage. Indeed, he appeared unable to look me in the eye or, I began to suspect, even properly locate me in the room.

"It's these glasses," he finally explained. "I've never been happy with them. However, let's proceed. I should take some details. Remind me of your surname."

"Peirce," I said.

"That's an odd coincidence, my name is Pearce too."

"How do you spell it?" I asked.

"P-E-A-R-C-E."

"Mine is spelt P-E-I-R-C-E," I said.

"Shouldn't that be P-I-E-R-C-E?" he said. "After all, i before e and all that?"

"It's a long story," I said.

"Still, how odd that we have names that sound the same even if spelled differently."

"A Homophonic Inexactitude," I told him. Then, in a sudden moment of insight, I asked, "The optician who prescribed your glasses – it wouldn't, by any chance, be the one in the High Street?"

"How on earth did you know that?"

As briefly as possible I outlined the theory that had suddenly leapt into my mind.

"Surely that's not likely?" was his reply.

I reached in my pocket for the broken spectacles I still carried.

"Try these on," I told him, "instead of the ones you're wearing."

He did so.

"My god!" he cried, suddenly seeing the world clearly for the first time. It must have been like a religious conversion for him.

Overall, I think, the therapist benefitted much more from the session than I did.

"How did that happen?" he asked, "two boys with almost identical surnames attending exactly the same optician, at exactly the same time and being given each other's spectacles?"

It probably won't surprise you to learn that my answer was: "Synchronicity."

Immediately afterwards the buzzer rang for the end of the session.

"That will be a hundred pounds," the therapist said. "I don't suppose I could keep the spectacles?"

"Of course. Will you take a cheque?"

"Of course."

I smiled. I knew he would never be able to cash it. Any cheque written by me would be refused by every bank.

I think he probably realised as much himself, once I passed it over. Possibly he decided not to make a point of it, since I had let him keep the spectacles.

"I can't help noticing," he said, studying the cheque, "you have a very interesting hand. Apart from being generally indecipherable, I see you do not indulge in ever crossing the *t's*."

SECOND PLACE

ONCE FOR FRIEND, TWICE FOR STRANGER

KAYLA MARTELL FELDMAN

My father used to say he had *real trouble remembering faces.*

I don't think I grasped his full meaning until the day Megan S. cut off my ponytail in the middle of a maths test as payback for not letting her copy my answers.

At the time, I wrote her off as a pathetic bully with a vengeance for smart kids, some cartoon character villain right out of a middle-grade straight-to-TV movie. Now I understand that she was probably just scared. The day she failed out of our class and was told she would have to retake the year, I caught her crying in the science block toilets.

Megan S. was given a three-day suspension for cutting off my hair and I spent the afternoon in the nurse's office as she tried desperately to fix the damage. As she ran her gnarled fingers through my golden locks, destroyed by the blunt scissors nicked from the art room, I remember thinking I should feel some sort of grief for the loss of three years' worth of hair growth. I loved my hair. My hair was glorious, gorgeous, godlike. But as I stared back at my reflection in the mirror, the nurse's panicked expression hovering anxiously above, I felt only a distant sense of relief. Something unlocked. After school, I went straight to the local Turkish barber and asked for a number two. When my father arrived home from work, set his keys into the dish by the door, and saw me standing at the end of the hall, he smiled.

"Are you a friend from school, then?" he asked.

The best part of prosopagnosia is that every time I look at her, I am struck, once again, by just how beautiful she is.

I was nineteen when I started having *real trouble* too.

Features began to slip from my memory until I could no longer call to mind the faces of my oldest friends. Later, a fellow graduate student working part-time in the library café had a nametag that read *Megan*, and I wondered faintly if she might be the same one whose future seemed dependent on the cleverness of a classmate. I took solace in the fact that so few of those people who shared my high school classrooms would recognise my adult body.

By the time I was twenty-five, I was meeting each friend anew. Every dinner party and cocktail catch-up, I was seeing their faces for the first time, listening hard for hints in their voices, searching for a familiar hairstyle or signature gait to tell me who was who. Harold had a speech impediment, that was easy. Alina had a lazy eye, which was simple enough until she invested in laser surgery and corrective glasses.

Somehow I got away with it. By being quiet, by listening, by paying attention to minute details. Freckles, slight differences in accents, favoured turns of phrase, the frequency with which certain names were mentioned.

My graduation was tricky. Matching caps and gowns and a majority white class of PhD candidates left my father grasping for clues. My hair was blue then, short and spiky, and when I saw him waiting at the gates to the hall where the ceremony would take place, I felt a pang of guilt for how often I felt the need to change my appearance. How many more adjustments he had had to make than any other parent of a child like me.

She was a blind date. Then again, all my dates are blind dates. Our mutual friend had sent me a photograph of her in advance, and I remember sitting at the bar, staring intently at that picture on my phone. I could have held it up beside its subject in person and would have had no way of knowing if they were the same.

I concentrate now on the softness of her fingers in the grooves of mine, the sweat on her palms. Her thumb moves over the back of my hand and she fiddles with my ring. A nervous habit. I feel that familiar spasm of guilt, for all the difficult things I have asked of her.

"There's some bruising around the jawline," the policeman says.

I turn, and his face is a puzzle I cannot solve.

She squeezes my hand once, which lets me know that this is a person I have met before. I look at his hands. Long piano fingers, no wedding band. *The same one who came to the house.*

One-night stands were a safe haven. No need to remember the face of someone you'll never see again. No obligation to stay the night or make breakfast in bed. Not after that first time, when I rolled over in the morning and panicked at the face of someone who could have been my next-door neighbour or my colleague or any number of people whose paths I had crossed before. Not after that first time, with the one who woke up angry.

"I'm not gay," he said, as he stuffed himself into his jeans.

I remember wondering why on earth he thought he might be.

After that, I decided I would tell them, before. Not that I *couldn't* remember but that I *wouldn't*. I said I liked it that way. That if we ever met again, it would be as strangers. I cannot say for certain that they all were.

Harold and Alina intervened eventually.

"It's not safe," they said. "We know you're lonely."

"I'm fine," I told them. "I like it this way."

But they knew, as old friends always do, that I wasn't, and I didn't.

They had fallen in love in that old-fashioned way of

pretending that they were just friends for nearly a decade before admitting, over a bottle of wine and a takeaway, that they had been in love for most of the time they had known each other.

The first time I saw her, there was not a doubt in my mind. I remember thinking that it would be impossible to forget that face. She looked nothing like her picture. Not that anyone does to me, but she was so much brighter, so much *more* in the flesh. She burst through the door in a yellow-scarved flurry, shaking snow out of the pockets of her coat. I marvelled at that smile. Then, as she lifted her scarf over her face, the slate was wiped clean again.

She wore her pronouns proudly on her coat beside a pink breast cancer pin and asked me for mine with my name. She told me what felt like everything she knew in its entirety on that first day and in every day that has followed I have been stunned by how much more she has had to tell me.

"Did you know," she said, the morning after our first date, drawing her finger gently from the centre of my forehead down the slope of my nose, "that you can tell a narwhal's past living conditions by its tusk?"

"I didn't know that."

"Yup," she grinned. "Just like the rings on a tree."

We fell asleep again after that, and there are no words for the panic that ripped through my gut when I wandered the flat after waking and discovered that she was gone. She was the first person I had allowed to spend the night in my bed since that first time, and I felt then the grief that I suppose I should have felt after that unwilling haircut from Megan S.

The bell rang, and I was still agonising over how I could have lost her so quickly when I answered the door, distraught and dishevelled. Stood on my doorstep was a yellow-scarved woman holding two cups of coffee.

"Narwhals also change colour with age," she said, and I burst into tears.

I sometimes wonder if my father never had more children because he feared he would mix them up. The first time I brought her home, he held her face in his and searched her eyes for something unforgettable, and found it.

He was overjoyed to have a daughter again.

In just six months she had slipped into my life so seamlessly, had met and memorised more faces and names than I thought possible even by people without this condition.

Her memory amazed me as she charmed her way through Christmases and birthdays and office parties, learning to sense my discomfort and ask all the right questions. *What was your name again? How do you know each other? And what do you do?* At my ten-year school reunion when someone sauntered over to say hello, nametag mercifully smoothed across her breast, I tensed as Megan S. reached for my hair, black then and shoulder-length.

"I was just awful back then," Megan laughed, leaning in to her. "I cut off all her hair with art scissors!"

She smiled back at Megan and gripped my arm.

"Their," she said simply, and whisked me away.

We were married that summer.

For my father's sake, we both wore white – she a dress, I a dinner jacket. We dressed our wedding party in matching yellow gowns with their names stitched into fabric at the collarbone, and Harold and Alina argued over who wore it best.

I wanted a small wedding, hoping to minimise the chance of me introducing myself to an aunt or cousin I'd known since birth, but her parents could not be stopped. We compromised on two hundred and fifty guests.

The system was her idea. One squeeze for my side, twice for hers. Before, during, and after the ceremony, her hand never left mine. *Once for friend, twice for stranger.*

We're in the room now, and her hand in mine is an anchor to everyone I ever meet.

The man is covered with a sheet, up to the neck. There is a purple bruise snaking up the right side of his jaw and up to his ear, just like the policeman said there would be. His hair is thinning, but it's not enough. There are no clues here, and I feel a sudden urge to whip the sheet away, to see the rest of his bare flesh and know if this man is who they think he is. But they trust that I would know his face.

He never took to anyone the way he did to her.

That house had not had a woman's laugh echo through its corridors since my mother, and now her laugh shook the walls with its thunderous joy.

My father had been lonely for longer than I can remember. Lonelier than I had ever been when sifting my way through feeble connections with the bodies of strangers, lonelier even than I had been as the weirdo at school in a skirt and a buzzcut and men's shoes. Not since I was born had my father risked bringing someone into his life whose face would fade.

And here he was, with the woman I loved, would love forever, sipping tea, telling her stories that only I knew, playing Scrabble, loving her as he had only ever loved me.

"Did you know," she said to him on his sixtieth birthday, grinning a sticky chocolate-cake grin, "that the severed head of a sea slug can grow a whole new body?"

I feel her fingers unlink from mine and she lets go of my hand.

In the end, there wasn't a choice. I remembered when I was a child, when his father died, asking mine where Grandpa had gone.

"Grandpas die, love. It's what they do."

It had been foolish to imagine that the magic of loving each other without giving him a grandchild might keep him alive forever.

We waited as long as we could, took care of him as best

we could, before there was no other option. He got sick and stayed sick, and it was only a few years before what he needed was far more than we were capable of giving.

While I filled out the forms, she squeezed my hand twice.

"He won't know who you are," I tried to explain to the new nurse. "You'll need to wear nametags and remind him constantly."

"We have a lot of residents who suffer from dementia," the nurse assured me.

Round the clock care, they said.

Locks on all the doors, they said.

The windows only open an inch, they said.

But still, he went wandering.

She has let go of my hand. She has let go of my hand and she is moving away from me. My lungs lurch and my heart tightens as I resist the urge to scream, because without her I am blind, without her hand to guide me they are all strangers, all mysteries waiting to be identified by a voice or a walk or a signature turn of phrase.

She sits on the stool beside him and I see that she is crying. She goes to move the sheet and I hear the policeman go to stop her, but then he doesn't. She has uncovered his hand. I watch as she takes that hand that is so often in mine, interlinks her fingers with his, and squeezes once.

"That's him," I tell the policeman. "That's my dad."

THIRD PLACE

SOMETIMES MY ANNOYING SISTER IS RIGHT

CATHERINE LEYSHON

What do you think of when you look at your feet? When I have the misfortune to glimpse mine, I think of hobbits: feet nearly as wide as they are long and toe-nails that no amount of nail varnish can beautify. And I'm going to have to get them out today, in public, in my local running shop.

I blame my sister, Erica. Serial overachiever. Ultra-marathon runner. In the great tombola of life, she got the legs of a giraffe, I got the physique of one of those old British Leyland Mini Mayfairs. By some tragic accident of genetics, she has the silky blonde hair of a unicorn, whereas my hair had gone the colour of the detritus in the vacuum cleaner bag by the time I was 35.

A couple of weeks ago, Erica had been banging on about a 64 mile race she was training for. I'd hesitate to drive 64 miles, let alone run them. While she'd sat there in her Sweaty Betty gear, talking about 'tapering', 'carbing up' and 'bonking', I'd been busy anaesthetising myself with wine. In the end I'd said – just to shut her up – "I'm doing Race for Life this year."

She nearly spat out her cauliflower, citrus peel and matcha powder smoothie. "You? Right!"

I swigged my own choice of health-giving drink, sauvignon blanc.

"I'm doing it for Mum and Auntie Sal." Saying it made it true, though I had only just thought of it. Even so, it felt right all of a sudden. Had it really been two years?

Far from shutting Erica up, my announcement only encouraged her to start talking about trainers like a scientist from Nike, oblivious to my Olympic-level eye-rolling. Next thing I knew, she'd bought me a voucher for something called 'gait analysis' and made me an appointment at the running shop in town. "Trust me," she had said. "This will change your life."

I've never been one to pass on a freebie so here I am, sitting on a foam cube next to a rack of exceedingly intimidating trainers. The running shop – Beast It – has posters of gorgeous women and men working out, looking delighted with themselves for being sweaty and energetic. And *young*, so young.

This is worse than the dentist.

Worse than a cervical smear test.

Worse than the menopause? Clearly that's ridiculous because there's nothing worse than the menopause. I don't want to think about all the things that have changed in the last five years, from my attention span (smaller) to my waistline (larger). And losing Mum and Auntie Sal came on top of all that.

And I'm single again. My choice. Ari turned out to be a git. But at least I'm not rattling around the house, looking at the gaps on the bookshelf where Ari's books used to be. I miss those books.

"Hi, I'm Huw," says a voice. "You're booked in for gait analysis, right?"

I look up. "Oh thank god, you're normal," I blurt.

Huw, a head taller than me, about my age, looks as if he's never run a yard in his life and I'm absolutely delighted about it. He's solid-looking enough but far from buff. He has one of those open, generous faces, full of perennial kindness. Bet he's nice to his mum.

"Normal? Well, it's all relative…" He looks at his clipboard. "…Bridget. Nice name. Celtic origins. Power, strength and virtue. They're quite the superpowers."

Huw's cheerfulness is, annoyingly, irresistible.

"Let's get started," he says. "Come into what I like to call The Lab."

I stand up reluctantly and follow him. "What are you going to do? Wire me up with electrodes, inject me with plutonium and give me bionic legs?"

"Exactly. It won't hurt a bit."

When I enter The Lab, I realise what gait analysis actually means. I'm required to run – *run*, for crying out loud – on a running machine whilst – and this is the really bad bit – *being filmed from behind.*

"It's filming your feet and your legs from the knees down, so I can see how you run," Huw says. "But I daresay once this footage hits YouTube, Martin Scorsese will be on the phone to your agent."

"Why? Is he casting the next superwoman film?" I ask. "Because I'm already booked as Scarlett Johansson's body double in her next movie."

Huw laughs. "Jump on. I'll start you at 5km/h and we'll take it from there."

I start walking. This is okay. I walked quite a lot when Ari and I were arguing all the time. Of course, once he'd gone, I spent a long time on the sofa with chocolate and wine positioned well within reach. So I'm a bit rusty, but I stick my shoulders back and march along briskly.

"What's your weekly mileage?" Huw asks.

"Zero. I won't lie, I had one too many glasses of sauvignon blanc and said I'd do Race for Life."

"Who hasn't done something daft after a glass of wine?"

I bet Huw hasn't. He doesn't look the type. But I appreciate the sentiment.

"I'm more of a chardonnay man myself," he says.

"Why? Did you have your tastebuds removed at birth?"

I realise I'm having fun. I don't think I've felt like this since dinosaurs roamed the earth. Admittedly my shins are killing me and the top of my leggings is starting to work its way past my muffin top, but I'm feeling pretty good.

"I don't even know how far the Race for Life is," I confess.

Huw disappears behind me to fiddle with the camera. "It's five kilometres."

I nearly fall off the running machine. "*How far?*"

"Just over three miles in old money." He reappears at the business end of the running machine. "Not that far."

Easy for him to say. He's not the one regretting their life choices.

"Camera's on." Huw presses buttons on the console of the running machine. "I'm going to nudge up the speed so that you're jogging."

I feel the belt go faster and my feet respond. Running to keep up has been the defining feature of my life for the past five years.

Huw is watching me jog. "What made you decide to start running?" he asks.

"I was trying to get my sister to stop talking about her next long run."

"I get it. Don't tell my boss, but runners can be really boring. Present company excepted."

"I'm not a runner," I pant.

"And yet here you are… running."

It's true, I'm actually *running*. And it's going okay, even though my boobs feel like a couple of out-of-control space hoppers. Note to self: must buy a sports bra if I'm going to go through with the madness of running 5k. Preferably one that has the structural integrity of London Bridge. If Erica could see me now, she'd be thrilled. And smug.

"So you're doing Race for Life," Huw says, sitting down on a folding chair. "I lost my mum to cancer."

I recognise something in his voice. I bet he doesn't say this out loud very often, or to many people. It's like he's still practising how to say it.

"Me too. Two years ago. And my Auntie Sal."

I jog on, filling the void by panting like an overweight labrador on a long walk on a hot day. It feels like we're sharing something without talking about what it is, because it's too monstrous and unfathomable, filling the space, drowning our hearts.

"Does it get easier, do you think?" Huw's voice is quiet.

"I'm probably not the right person to ask. All I know is that no matter how much you want the world to stop spinning, it just keeps going. And not only that, it seems to get faster and faster. A bit like this running machine."

"Oh sorry!" Huw leaps up and presses the buttons that slow things down again.

I'm a sweaty mess. Even my eyelids are sweating.

"Well done," Huw says. "You survived that. Nobody had to call an ambulance."

"Not yet, anyway," I gasp.

He shows me the footage from the camera on a laptop.

"There you are," he says. "Classic mid-foot strike. Nice gait. You could run forever."

"I'll take your word for it."

Huw hands me a bottle of water. "Let's get you into some running shoes. I'll find a convenient skip for the ones you're wearing now."

The moment we shared in The Lab has gone, but it's

left a residue, a connection. I sit back down on a foam cube and Huw fetches a wobbling tower of shoe boxes.

I'm wearing the trainers I do the gardening in along with my best – indeed, my only – sports socks. Marks and Spencer. I bought them on the way to the running shop after realising that my calf-length socks adorned with gambolling sausage dogs were probably not sending the right signals. I sit down, kick off my trainers and start to peel off the first of my immaculate white socks, anticipating that Huw will faint away at the sight of my feet.

He holds up a hand. "Woah, Bridget. No need to strip off. We've only been friends for five minutes. You can leave your socks on for this bit."

Huw sits on the floor in front of me and takes my left foot in one hand. He puts his thumb right in my arch and gives it a rub. It feels electrifyingly good. Not-exactly-buff Huw from the running shop might have hidden talents.

"Got to look after your arches," he says. "I'm going to put you in a trainer with some cushioning."

He opens boxes, discards the first few trainers, then produces a radioactive blue pair. When I put one on, it feels like a slipper, hugging my foot. He checks the fit, holding my ankle in one hand and squeezing my foot with the other. It's quite delicious. If I'd known this is what getting fitted for a pair of trainers feels like, I would've pretended to like running years ago.

"I'll pop the other trainer on you and we'll go back in The Lab and have another go on the running machine."

"You could do Race for Life with me," I say suddenly. I even take myself by surprise. "For your mum."

Huw looks up at me from where he's lacing the other trainer. He's got an irresistible warmth, like the best cardigan you ever had, the one you wrap yourself in when you come in from walking the dog, you're soaked to the skin, and it's time for a massive glass of red wine and a true-crime drama on the telly.

"Do they let blokes do it?"

I nod. "Pink wigs and all."

Huw sits back on his heels. "I haven't run in ages. I sort of stopped when mum died. Started cultivating the old snack area instead." He slaps his tummy.

I nod. It gets in the way, grief. My own snack area has been on a vigorous expansion programme of its own. "We've got ten weeks though – more than enough time."

What am I saying?

But Huw smiles at me, delighted, and it's like we've somehow managed to stumble into exactly the right person at exactly the right time.

"Look," Huw says, "I get off in half an hour. Let's get your trainers sorted, then I'll let you buy me a coffee and I'll talk you through a training plan we can use."

I catch sight of the price label on the nearest shoe box. "I'm about to spend £110 on a pair of trainers and you'll let *me* buy *you* a coffee?"

"Tell you what. I'll give you a staff discount on the trainers, and then I'll let you buy me lunch." And he heads off towards The Lab.

"How is that better, Huw? How?" I call after him. But we're both grinning.

"Come on," Huw says. "Hurry up. I'm hungry."

What did Erica say? This would change my life. So annoying when she's right.

HIGHLY COMMENDED

AS ABOVE, SO BELOW

LAURA TIMMS

About 1783, another member of the family took in two acres of moor on the north side of the Inn. His pioneering but unsuccessful effort to grow wheat and potatoes, at 1325 feet above sea level, gained him a modest immortality.

The History of The Lion Inn, Blakey Ridge by J.H. Ruston

Above

The bloody rotten scabby-faced bugger scuttles about inspecting his plots as Annie watches him, scoured by the wind. He marked out the moor, measuring and calculating. Now, scraping down through ashy peat, what does he expect to find there? They have bread.

He writes notes in his book, draws careful pictures

of lumpy potatoes, although takes no note of those she cooks to feed him. He has told her the King of Sweden himself has decreed that cultivation of potatoes must increase. Indeed, he tells her that in that country, men of genius have learned how to make potato brandy.

What Annie knows of Sweden is what she knows of the world – flotsam and jetsam from fishermen, whalers, ships – sea-work. She looks past her stooping husband, now close to the soil, examining. She cannot see the sea here at the top, although it is so high up under this cold heaven, she feels the wind could blow her to the sea again, if only a gust were strong enough. What does she care for the King of Sweden?

Annie has a heart of salt for her husband. She wants no part of his enterprise.

Middle

Annie keeps at her work as her husband keeps at his. They eat; he is busy. Days continue. In the dark soil, it may be that seeds and tubers are at their work of sprouting.

Her husband paces, checks, watches the land as if scanning the sea to glean what swims beneath. Seeds and shoots sprout slowly, if they sprout at all. Annie misses the silver flash of fish. The sea is wide and it is not the habit of fish to build a house and live in it.

Annie's husband writes and receives letters. His project is a curiosity to others. He finds this interest enlivening;

Annie had not thought he could be busier. He bustles around his plot where nothing grows, now measuring rainfall, recording in his book, poking at the soil. He does not have an instrument to measure the shortness of Annie's patience, but perhaps he feels it.

Annie's teeth ache with bad temper bitten down on. The flesh of her face sparks and crackles under her skin, rage burrowing through her, hollowing her out. Annie has heard old stories of this land once being laid waste, of revenge on the North, starvation and salted earth. On the moor top, only heather grows, billowing in every direction. It still seems a waste to Annie, but her anger is so hot inside her that those old stories of hunger and slaughter have a wicked charm. There is satisfaction in feeling so very angry, in imagining everything destroyed.

Annie's husband's mind is full of hope and growth. He is entranced by vegetable possibility.

Below

This project of wheat and potatoes has always seemed to Annie a fool's errand, one in which she is yoked to the fool. Caught up in the net of her fury, contempt blinds her to her husband and the course of his endeavour. John's excitement, his plans, his visions are sprouting, tangling, surging. He walks faster, checks more often, writes longer, sleeps less. He begins to talk to himself, to address an empty room as if it were the Royal Society. His life is thrilling. Each day he feels he could burst in anticipation of the first shoots appearing. His mind dances. He forgets that Annie is there at all. She does not notice.

One morning Annie wakes; as usual, John is not there. In the course of her morning duties, she glances out towards his plots. She cannot see him. Annie looks more closely. She makes out John, face down on the bare earth – for a moment, she thinks, *Is he trying to plant himself?*

Annie rushes towards him, ready to scold. She draws nearer; John is plunging his hands into the soil, face caked in dirt. Exhilarated, he sees Annie, flings soil and fragile sprouts towards her. See, Annie! They're growing!

Annie steps to meet him, earth turned to water beneath her. All around John, all around her, the seedlings and shoots that John has watched and longed for have been pulled up. See Annie! They're growing! I've made them grow!

Annie stares at vegetable possibility withering before her. The tiny plants, uprooted, now as sickly and desperate as fish out of water. Annie is from and of the sea. It has its own harsh wisdom. In her village, it is bad luck to save a drowning man. It seems to her that John has drowned in earth.

Annie turns her back on John and sets off, down from the moor top, back towards the booming and roaring of the sea.

HIGHLY COMMENDED

EROSION
PENNY BLACKBURN

The sea took a bite last night.

A big one, bigger than I've seen for a couple of years. The last big one stopped the Asda delivery man in his tracks, shouting over the gap where the road used to be.

"I'll have to leave it here, mate. Can you manage?"

"Aye."

I'll admit, it was a struggle. Had to make four trips on the mobility scooter, but I got everything back to the bungalow myself. Never needed help from anyone and, at my age, it's no time to start asking. Since then I've used the village shop, edging the scooter along the thin strip of tarmac which remains, trying not to look down at the sheer drop to the beach below. I just get a few bits as I need them. Not needed a lot since Lizzie… not that she ate much, but she was a bugger for puddings.

The chunk that's gone this morning is further up, away

from the village and near the caravan park – which they've had to move again, but hardly anyone keeps a static there anymore. That young feller who runs it, the one with the dog that follows him everywhere, he says people are too scared to sleep there now. Frightened they'll be taken by the sea during the night and end up at the bottom of the cliff. *Some of them could do with it*, I think, as he's talking. Get rid of their noisy kids and their stinking barbecues – there's nowt appetising about half burnt, half raw meat in my opinion.

Lizzie did the best roast, none of this pink-in-the-middle rubbish you get now. I remember when we went to that fancy pub in the village, treated ourselves to a Sunday dinner. We couldn't eat the meat, except round the edges. Lizzie looked embarrassed, told the waiter, "We're just a bit full, love." The waiter didn't comment on how she still managed to get a hefty portion of crumble and custard down. We said next time we'd have the chicken, but somehow we never got back there.

•

I hate the sound of the sea now. That ever-present hush-shush, hush-shush as it breathes in and out down there on the beach.

Sometimes the wind gets up and it whips round the walls and rattles the roof tiles – a good few want fixing now, but there doesn't seem much point. At least a howling wind blocks out the sound of the sea for a while.

The constant noise of the surf used to reassure me when we first moved here – back when I retired and we thought this place was perfect. We loved it so much we ignored the red flags on the survey, thought it'd never happen to us. There was forty feet between us and the edge, and another bungalow. We didn't know that one was already empty and unsellable, didn't realise there'd been another one beyond it which had already fallen.

I go to make a cuppa. It's not the same these days, the bags are a funny shape – what was wrong with proper square ones? I'd make a pot, but it's a waste just for one. The nearest cup in the cupboard is the god-awful one with a squint-eyed cat under a weird kind of flower that never existed on this earth. Lizzie loved it, said it made her laugh. I'm sure I shoved it to the back a couple of days ago. Sick of seeing it. I definitely push it right to the back now, behind the fancy ones we got for our wedding. Never used them – Lizzie kept them for best. I drag one out now. I guess they might as well get some use.

Thing is, I thought I'd got rid of everything after she'd gone. All her clothes – shoes and skirts and blouses and handbags, her bits of fancy jewellery that she never really wore, her books and make up and the half bottle of that perfume she always dabbed on – not quite apple, not quite pear. "*Quince*, Frank," she'd tell me every time I mentioned it. "Like in the Owl and the Pussycat." I'd pull her close, then, for a dance. We'd laugh and she'd whisper "Hand in hand…" But the edge of the sand got too close after we moved here, and we stopped doing that.

All gone. Chucked in black bags and carted off to the charity place. Janet from the shop backed the little van up as far as she could to the lip of the collapsed tarmac and her kids came up to the bungalow to collect everything.

Janet said, "Are you sure, Frank? It's very soon."

But I wanted it gone, couldn't bear to look at it all. I thought that cup had gone too, but I must have missed it. My mind isn't what it was, I get forgetful about things. My age is starting to show and in a way I'm glad Lizzie isn't here to see it. Ten years between us never seemed that much, but as we got older I started to feel it more. She was still so full of life and fun and I was stuck trundling along on the mobility scooter. If I'd been spry enough to follow her that day…

•

What was it the council said in that letter? *The interpretative conclusions of the cost-benefit analysis indicate…* A fancy way of saying 'We're doing nowt'. Apparently if they put up any kind of sea defence, some poor buggers further down the coast will be washed away. And we've no hope of compensation – with all the cuts, the council's strapped for cash and there's no value for *them* in buying land that won't be here in a few years. Even the insurers have given up on us. It's a bad job when those grabbing buggers won't take your money. I just hope this place can hold on until I'm gone.

We came here on a wave of nostalgia and longing.

We were both brought up inland – Lizzie's first visit to the seaside was when she was seventeen. I went as a boy – packed off from Manchester to some distant cousins in the North East while my mum was ill. I remembered scrambling up and down the cliffs and digging in the soft, golden sand. We didn't realise how the coastline changes around the country – none of those firm sandstone crags round here. Here, it's soft clay – 'till' they call it – which was dumped by glaciers. Borrowed land, and the sea wants it back.

We just needed to move, after all the carry on… a new home and a new start. We looked all over and couldn't believe the prices, even for somewhere so small you couldn't turn round without bumping into yerself. When we found this beauty in our price range, we were chuffed. We didn't question why properties here were so much cheaper.

We didn't know the history of buildings lost over the edge. About a year before we came here, the Warden Tower went over. Janet told me about it, said her dad used to take her there when she was little, and she gestured out at a space above the sea which now only exists in her memory. I could see the stones half-buried on the beach.

"Gone," she said. "Overnight." I heard the catch in her voice and patted her arm gently. It's hard to see something you love broken at the bottom of a slump of earth and rock.

•

That bloody cup! I must be really losing it. I could have sworn I put it to the back of the cupboard and there it is on the drainer. Lizzie used to annoy me by leaving her dirty cup on there. That's the clean side – why couldn't she put it on the other side of the sink? And she used to leave an inch of tea in the cup, I could never see why.

"Shall I only make you half a cup?"

"Don't be daft, then it wouldn't be full enough."

I let out a huff – half laugh, half irritated – at the memory. But I'm unsettled. Surely I'm not *that* doolally yet? For there's an inch of tea at the bottom. My stomach flips and I shake a little as I quickly tip the tea out, rinse the cup. On impulse I throw it into the bin, shove it down under the ready meal cartons and plastic wrapping.

"Pull yourself together, man," I whisper to myself. It feels for a moment like the sea pauses, listens for a response, before it continues its war of attrition against the base of the cliffs.

•

It's been two days since the Bite, as everyone here refers to it, but I can't help feeling there's more to come. When there's a big event – huge landslides and structures falling into the sea – it makes the evening news and there are dramatic pictures in the local paper for a week or so. But the smaller slips are just as dangerous. That big slip a couple of years ago came after a week of storms. Everyone can imagine the wild sea lashing against the friable cliffs and grabbing handfuls of coastline, but it's too easy to forget that after a few days of unrelenting rain, even when the sun shines, the earth is saturated.

That feller at the inquest said it: "An increased volume of rainfall increases the weight of the land as it pushes down on its own weakened roots. A person might not realise that the additional pressure of an angry footstep can be the trigger for another slice of cliff to shear away."

For a moment, I'm sure I can feel the floor shift under me. I'm starting to think it's a question of whether I outlast the house, or the house outlasts me. I took a look outside this morning, went round to the sea-facing side – which I try not to do if I can help it. The forty feet we started out with has been eaten away to less than four.

I looked at the sea and tried to throw my anger at it. But the sea doesn't take any blame. How can it? Did the sea shout at her that day, tell she was a disgrace for flirting with the waiter?

"For goodness sake, Frank! I'm nearly sixty-five – why would you be jealous of a teenager?"

"Because, of course, I've never had any reason to be jealous."

"No, you haven't, Frank. You didn't then and you don't now. I thought when you moved me here to the arse-end of nowhere, you'd be happy. I thought we were going to put all that behind us."

I knew she was right, but I couldn't back down. She slammed her cup down – tea sloshing out and over the grinning cat – and marched out of the house. As soon as the door banged shut, I wished I could take it all back. I would've gone after her, but I knew I'd never catch her on my blasted scooter. "I'll say sorry when she comes back," I told myself, as I watched her through the window, stomping across the cliff top. Then I turned away.

•

I've been putting off going into the kitchen. I've tidied the rest of the house, put all the laundry away and changed the bed. I'm not sure there was much point, but it felt right. Now I'm just sitting watching the last lines of red bleed out of the sky.

I suppose it's time. I flick the light on as I enter the kitchen and when my eyes adjust, I'm not surprised by what I see: the cup is in the middle of the table, clean and waiting for a fresh brew.

I feel the bungalow tremble around me, feel the floor buck and I fall to my knees. A strong scent hits my nostrils and my brain takes less than a second to recognise it. *Quince*, I think, as the world slides from under me.

HIGHLY COMMENDED

MY NIGEL

PATRICK BELSHAW

He wasn't what you'd call a handsome man, my Nigel. His nose was too big, for one thing. Big, and rather beaky. And his eyes, though bright, were too far apart.

But what he lacked in looks, he made up for in length. Because he was tall, my Nigel. Six feet five in his stockinged feet. And that's tall from where I'm standing.

"He seems to go up and up for ever!" our Mam said, the first time she clapped eyes on him. I can see her now, her neck stretched, her head tilted backwards. "Fair gives me an 'eadache, just looking up at 'im."

Mind, she was only four foot ten, our Mam. A little dot of a thing. "Like a doll in a box," we said, when we saw her laid out in that funeral parlour. It's her I take after. Because I'm a bit on the small side myself.

'The stork and the sparrow' they called us, me and my Nigel. And I suppose we must have looked a bit comical walking down the street together, me coming just a few inches above his belly-button. You could see folk trying to hide their smiles, and you couldn't blame them really. They'd be wondering – like you, I guess – how we ever came together in the first place.

Well, we met in the waiting room at the vet's. Nigel sat nursing a bird with a damaged wing, and I was cradling a sick puppy inside my coat. It was funny, because he didn't strike me as being all that tall at first. But when he unwound his legs and got to his feet – wow! His head was almost brushing the ceiling. And that was it. I've always had a weakness for tall men.

It was the opposite for him, of course. He liked things small. To him, I was probably like one of them dinky novelties you find in Christmas crackers. And like all novelties, it didn't take long before the shine wore off me.

I shouldn't have been surprised, really. We just weren't compatible. It had nothing to do with sex; neither of us knew what the fuss was about there. Sex is vastly overrated, if you ask me – although I have to admit we did try it a few times when we were first married.

I don't think I ever really got the urge, that was the problem. Not properly, anyway. Not like they reckon you should in all the magazines. And as for Nigel – well, he never seemed to find the energy somehow.

"Well, what can you expect?" our Mam said, not looking the slightest bit surprised. "A bolted onion, that's your Nigel! Poor chap's outgrown his strength."

He may not have been handsome, my Nigel, but at least

he was tall and dark. A bit on the slender side, perhaps. For his height. Skinny, even, some might have said. And although he had long dark hair, it was a sort of dull-black colour – like that big bible Nana used to get down for us kids to swear on. That's probably why he used to try and shiny it up with Brylcreem.

Brylcreem couldn't disguise the dandruff, though. Suffered from dandruff something chronic, my Nigel. Tried everything to shift it. Like a chemist's shop, our bathroom cabinet used to be. They smelt horrible, as well, the special potions he used. Strong as lavatory cleaner, some of them. And still his dandruff fell. Like snowflakes. You'd see it settling on his collar. Even on his shoulders, sometimes. Well, when he was sitting down, you would. Perhaps that was why he didn't sit around much. Except in his own room. Just didn't want people to notice.

He was always on the go, my Nigel. As soon as he came in from work, he'd have a quick cuppa and then he'd be off out again. Out to meet his birds. In his aviary, I mean. Out in the back garden. And oh, it did annoy me. Not just because he seemed to prefer their company to mine, but mainly because I hate to see birds in cages.

"You – of all people!" I used to go on at him. "How can you? Call yourself an orni-what'sit… bird fancier, bird lover… whatever? How can you take little creatures that God gave wings to – creatures that are meant to fly free in the air – and lock them up in cages?"

Oh, I did use to give him what for, I can tell you. But he would just look down at me, my Nigel, and say – ever so quietly, ever so mildly, give him credit – "The better to study them, my dear. The better to get to know their little ways. And although I take your point, you have to remember that my birds were born and raised in captivity. They don't know any different. If I set them free, they wouldn't last five minutes out there in the big, bad world."

And he was probably right. After all, he was the expert. Knew far more about birds than I did. Far more about everything, for that matter. When he wasn't out there with his birds, he'd be up there in his room with his beaky nose stuck in some book or other, usually one about birds. He especially loved to read about their migration habits.

"One of the wonders of nature," he used to say, blinking, giving me that *wise old owl* look of his, "the way they find their way here, year after year, from all those exotic places."

And I'd feel like saying, "Yes, dear – but not *your* birds. Six thousand miles…? More like six feet for your poor little buggers! For them, the only wonder is they don't die of boredom." But I would never have said such things. What would have been the point – ruffling his feathers, upsetting him like that? I had enough long silences to cope with as it was.

Oh, how he would have loved to travel to them places, my Nigel.

"Just imagine!" he would cry, clapping his hands at the ends of his long arms, which would beat almost like wings themselves. "Imagine following the white stork to Africa, the pectoral sandpiper to the Arctic tundra, the white-fronted goose to the wastes of Siberia…" Oh, he did go on! "…or, better still, the Arctic tern all the way to the frozen seas of Antarctica. Imagine that. Even the shorter journeys – like the redwings and the fieldfares, winging off to Scandinavia. Yes – given the chance, I'd follow any of them anywhere."

When I took his tea up to his room, I would often find him poring over that big atlas of his, looking all them places up. And he would receive the mug from me – sometimes without a word, as if I was a servant: that did annoy me – before going back to his maps, or losing himself in one of his many travel books.

But it was no good him dreaming. He could never travel to such places, my Nigel. Except in his mind, in his imagination. *Such a shame!* I thought, smiling secretly to myself.

It wasn't the money. Not really – although he couldn't have gone anywhere on what he earned at the bakery. My part-time job at the vet's could have made a difference, except I spent all my earnings on clothes and accessories. Mad about clothes, I am. Always have been.

"And why not?" I used to argue. "You've got your precious birds. You don't think twice about spending money on them. A woman's got to have some sort of interest – especially when her husband hardly seems to notice her."

He had no answer to that. He knew I was right, even if he didn't want to admit it.

No, it wasn't the cash. I wouldn't fly, you see, that was

the problem. And I wouldn't travel by boat, either. I hated water. Just wouldn't go on it – or too near it, for that matter. It wasn't so much that I was frightened, it was simply that I suffered terrible travel sickness. The slightest movement, the merest vibration – and that was it for me. I'd go green at the gills. And my poor guts! Turn themselves inside out, they would.

I was just as bad in cars. Almost, anyway. Trains as well, really – although I did cope a bit better by rail. At least on a train you can get up and walk about a bit.

Poor Nigel! Imagine his frustration. He was a martyr to my weakness, poor dear. One train ride somewhere once a year, with me looking miserable and throwing up half the time – and that was his lot! He'd be thinking of all those exotic places he was forever going on about – and all he got was a trip to Scarborough. Not much for the imagination to play with there – although, come to think of it, he at least had plenty of seagulls to keep him happy, whereas I just had two hellish journeys, with hours of boredom sandwiched in between.

I didn't feel the slightest bit sorry for him, mind. In fact, to tell you the truth, I was secretly pleased to have a really good excuse for not travelling to all them foreign parts – where, let's be honest, he'd have spent all his time on his precious birdwatching, leaving me to twiddle my thumbs as usual. Either that, or he'd be hours swimming about in some warm sea somewhere, while I looked on, getting sun-burnt.

He was fond of swimming, my Nigel. Had the feet for

it, you see. Huge, they were, his feet. Like great paddles. Not only that – they were webbed! It's true, the second and third toes on each foot were joined together by flaps of skin. Looked really weird, they did. A bit like a frog's feet. Made cutting his nails difficult. That's why he got me to do it – and ugh, it used to turn my stomach over, handling them big, sweaty, freaky feet of his.

He found swimming easy, of course. Well, he would, wouldn't he? With feet like a duck – or like one of them diving birds he was always going on about. Yes, he took to water like a fish, my Nigel. He could spend hours in it. "You'll turn into one, one day," I used to say. And then I'd go on to joke about it...

"One of your little brothers for tea today, Nigel!" I'd say, as I served him a bit of cod or smoked haddock. And when he started to eat, I'd tap him on the wrist with my fork and say, "Cannibal! Don't know how you could. Have you no conscience?"

He didn't do much swimming on that last holiday we had together, mind. Sea too cold, for one thing. July, it was – but talk about cold! Like winter, it was, on that caravan site near Robin Hood's Bay, with the wind so strong it nearly cut you in half. Didn't seem to bother my Nigel, though. He just pulled on that tatty old bird-watching anorak of his, and off he went, the yellow pom-pom on his woolly hat bob-bob-bobbing up and down, like a beacon going on and off, warning the fishermen out at sea.

It was only our second full day. We'd got there late

in the afternoon on the Saturday, you see, and we'd spent most of Sunday getting our bearings and learning the ropes. There was a lot to take in; we'd never hired a caravan before.

But, first thing Monday morning, there he was, my Nigel, true to form, all organised, ready and rearing to go. Off along the cliffs towards Ravenscar he strode, map in one hand, binoculars in the other, little knapsack on his big, broad back, to do a bit of bird watching. Didn't even wave goodbye – which was sad, really, because that was the last I saw of him.

They never found his body. *Missing, presumed drowned…* that was the coroner's verdict, weeks later.

I've been out here two or three times since – up here on the high cliffs above the Wykes, near where he was last seen. And as I look out to sea, I often wonder what might have happened to poor Nigel. I'm not grieving, if that's what you're thinking. Nothing like that. In fact, to be honest, I haven't enjoyed life as much for years.

No, I just like it up here, that's all. Feel a sense of freedom, if you want to know. Don't mind the sea so much these days, either. And I'm not nearly as travelsick as I used to be. Why, one day soon, I might even risk a flight to Spain. Fancy a bit of sun on my back. And who knows, I might get off with one of them Spanish waiters. Might even find that missing urge! You never know.

Oh, look! There's that cormorant again. Keeps taking off and landing on Eel Rock, that flattish rock just to the left of Low Nab Point. Quite comical, really. Almost as if it's new-fangled with its wings. Strange – it reminds me of Nigel, somehow. He liked black. Hardly wore anything else. And oh, he did love his birds.

He loved fish, too.

SHORTLISTED STORIES

THE DAY THE SPINACH WILTED

JENNY ADAMTHWAITE

Because it happened on a Sunday, a lot of people thought it was an act of God. All the spinach in the fields had wilted as though the earth had sucked out its water with a drinking straw, and in the graveyard behind the fields, the ground had all cracked like it does in hot places on the TV. Ella's dad had shown her pictures. He'd come back early from the farm where you pick your own vegetables because you can't pick droopy spinach, even though it goes droopy when you cook it anyway.

"Climate change," he said, which is more or less what he said about everything. It was a bit like how Molly's mum said that God works in mysterious ways every time something inconvenient happened: it made sense to a point, but really it was just a thing grownups said to make things make sense when they didn't.

The day the spinach wilted, Ella's dad took her into town to get a sausage sandwich from the market. They did it every Sunday. Sometimes they'd see people going into church, and her dad would laugh like he knew something they didn't. But he didn't. Everybody knew that the sausage queue was shorter before the church service finished. Afterwards, she'd sit on the monument, dangling her legs and eating her sandwich while he went to get a newspaper and whatever they'd run out of at home, which was usually milk because no one ever remembered to buy enough milk. She liked to listen to the conversations everyone in the square was having and eat around the edge of her bun so that by the time she got to the middle, the bread had gone all squishy and pink with ketchup, and you couldn't tell where the bread ended and the sausage began.

All anyone was talking about was spinach. It was quite boring really because no one knew why it had happened, but everyone had an opinion. They were worried about the gravestones, but not for any real reason other than they thought dead people should be respected. She nibbled around her bun and wondered what people would say if something really interesting happened – like aliens or talking dogs.

"Hello," said a boy, pulling himself up beside her. He was grubby and dressed like he was playing an olden days' chimney sweep in a school play.

"Hello," she said. "What do you think about the spinach? Actually, never mind. That's boring. What do you think it feels like to have wings?"

The boy shrugged. "I think the spinach was something to do with me. I think I needed water."

"I'm Ella," she said.

"I'm Charlie. I'm not cold. That's odd, isn't it?"

Ella nodded. She had her big scarf on, and she'd be wearing her gloves if she wasn't eating a sausage sandwich. Charlie was wearing trousers that stopped at the knees and his sleeves were rolled up.

"Do you think heaven's real?" he asked.

Ella stopped chewing for a second so she could concentrate on thinking.

"My dad says the stars are bright enough to light your way if it is, but it's probably not, so we don't have to worry about believing in God." She took another bite of her sandwich, and a blob of ketchup landed on her jeans. "What do you think?"

"I expect it's real. I expect this is a mistake and God will sort it all out."

"Are you meant to be dead?"

Charlie kicked his legs and stared down at his shins. "I had polio. I couldn't walk."

"I broke my leg when I was little. I could still walk though. I just had to have crutches."

"I think maybe I should wait in the graveyard. Or at the church. What do you think would be better? If heaven is real."

Ella swallowed the last bit of sausage, which she'd got wrong because she wasn't concentrating properly. There should have been more bread than that for the last bite.

"Maybe the graveyard. You'd be able to see the stars better. I could bring you a cheese sandwich if you get hungry."

Charlie looked like he was thinking very hard, and then he said, "I don't think I will. You know how you feel like you're hollow when you're hungry? I don't feel like that anymore."

"I could bring you a blanket for if you get cold while you're waiting."

"I don't think I'll need that either." Charlie thought for a while, kicking his legs and watching his knee caps. "Maybe you could bring me a candle though. I don't like the dark."

When she went home, Ella found him a torch and took it to the graveyard behind the spinach fields. At bedtime, she watched the light flicker around the graves and wondered what would happen. If he wasn't there in the morning she'd have to start believing in heaven. And if he was, she supposed he'd have to come to school. She wondered if he knew anything about fractions.

In the morning, the spinach was all fixed and the ground was wet, and Charlie wasn't anywhere to be seen. Her dad went to the farm after work and they had spinach with their tea, cooked until it was droopy and dark. Wasn't she supposed to believe in heaven now? She wasn't sure she did. Probably Charlie was just dead again like before.

WHEN THE LOVELINESS OF LADYBIRDS LANDED

HELEN VICTORIA ANDERSON

There was that summer when playtimes and dinnertimes seemed to last forever and the sky was holiday-brochure blue. As soon as her class was released via the Junior School door, Hazel would shake off the swarm and dash towards the wooden perimeter fence. Out there, she took up her position, lying on her tummy on the cool, bouncy grass. She liked to arch her neck and squint through the gaps between the slats to see what her favourite families in the neighbouring houses were up to. A lady with curlers in her fringe, washing up at the sink behind a cute little window framed with frilly curtains. A jolly, reddening baby sprinkling water into a crate of stony sand borrowed from the beach. A bristle-faced man who must be the dad – though he looked nothing like her own – slumping in a green striped deckchair and taking sharp puffs from a shrinking cigarette. She liked to give them names and lives.

When they were out of view, or she had almost been seen, Hazel would rotate towards the Infant School building and try to whistle through a slit in a blade of grass. Hazel sometimes made daisy-chains. She wanted to make a magnificent necklace that would wipe the smirks off the other girls' faces but her patience always ran out before she'd even achieved a passable bracelet. Then, she would snap the wilted stems and pluck the drooping petals and dig her nail into the spongy centre because the boys wouldn't let her play football and the girls called her Swot and she wondered if pretty things hurt, too. Hazel dreamed of fooling someone – anyone – in her class with a convincing four-leaf clover fashioned from entwined, mutilated three-leafers.

Out there, by the fence, she would worry at the grazes and stains on the knees that her grandma had called "solid", dreading the extra scrubbing that would come her way in that evening's bath. Hazel liked to peel down her once-white socks to admire the lacy pink pinpricks branded on her fuzzy shins by the sun. On the rare days when the sky was interrupted, she would press her back to the earth and look upwards. She shielded her eyes from the remaining glare with a wonky salute so that she could scan the clouds for animal outlines and God looking down from Heaven like he did in her Illustrated Bible. She could hear the other children squealing and chanting, but Hazel had better games, like guessing how many seconds would pass until the sun would be blotted out – how long before it would creep out and the world would be shiny again – by gauging the strength and direction of the sea breeze on her licked, bitten forefinger.

Once the days of unexpected heat turned into weeks, the news on Dad's telly was full of warnings. In English, they learnt how to spell 'drought'. In Science, they learnt that good weather can be bad. Out there, on the school field, after school dinner, Hazel liked to entice ladybirds to land in the palms of her hands. She assigned them characters and histories, coaxing them to crawl across her heart- and life-lines by using a sweet voice that the boys and girls would not have recognised as hers. She bristled against the tickle of their legs and bellies on her rough skin as she counted their dots, prizing the ladybirds with the reddest and glossiest wings.

Hazel pitied the unripe tomato-coloured inferiors. She also hated them, like she hated girls who kept creatures in jars with breathing-holes gouged in the lid as an afterthought. She let the ladybirds crawl up the pale insides of her wrists towards the outstretched crook of her elbow. Free. She would watch for the tell-tale signs of their waxy wings parting and lifting and she would be alone and lonely again. But better to have loved and lost, like her grandma said. Nothing lasts forever, no matter how hard you pray or wish or promise to be good.

Dad's paper pronounced a plague, stamping its pages with blurry pictures of sad allotment-men who had managed to grow something – anything – in their parched plots, only for the spotty blighters to chomp it right away into nothing. By the end of term, every single ladybird that landed on Hazel was a monster, twice or three times as big as the ones she had loved weeks earlier. There was no cajoling now. They wriggled down the collar of her school blouse, front and back. They caught in the rats' tails of her long brown hair and thrashed around until they made cotters. Still, she tried to tease them out and let them go without squishing them.

By now, they were biting, leaving tiny, burning wounds. The boys liked to point at the welts on her neck and tell true stories of millions of ladybirds hatching under your skin. The girls called her Spot. She tried not to pick. Hazel had to abandon her families through the fence. She liked to think they would sense that something – someone – was missing. The grass on the field was crunchy and brown. By now, she had lost count of the seconds – the minutes, hours, and days – since a cloud had crossed the sky.

Hazel spent playtimes and dinnertimes crouched in the dust-dabbed shade behind the mesh under the pre-fab classrooms. She liked to scratch the names of the meanest boys and girls in the dirt with the tips of her once-black school shoes and imagine the trouble they'd be in with the caretaker. She liked to try to not think about armies of spotty blighters advancing through her veins and eating away at her brain. She would watch the shimmering outline of the teacher patrolling the playground for signs of them, preparing to lift a dazzling whistle to their lips. Then, Hazel would put on her shell, scuttle back into the open, and walk sensibly inside, just like all the other children.

STRANGERS
ARTEMIS

"We could make this work," he insisted.

She offered him a sad smile.

He placed his hands on her shoulders, wanting to shake her but holding back. "Why? Why won't you just give me a chance?"

She didn't say anything. Her coffee cup sat on the table, souring with cold.

He tried again, gentler, noticing her stiffness. "Remember that time on the beach after our college graduation? There was that bonfire and our song – our song! – was playing and we snuck off to watch the moonrise and it was perfect. It was perfect."

"That was a good night."

"Good! It was *amazing*." His declaration came out louder than expected, and the other customers in the café turned their heads. He didn't waste time blushing. Quieter, he reiterated, "It was really amazing. That was the best night of my life and–"

"Would you like to order anything else today?" the waitress interrupted.

"No," the two of them said at once.

The waitress nodded and departed briskly.

The man looked at the woman and ran a hand through his hair. Hidden safely under the veil of his shoes, his toes danced a sporadic rhythm. He continued, "I wake up every morning and I kick myself because I'm not living that life anymore. I want that again."

She pursed her lips.

When it became clear he wasn't getting his point across to her, he made a point to sit down next to her instead.

They stared at each other. She didn't speak. He wanted to say more, but he'd said enough. *Why won't she say anything?* Then, she did. "It's been twenty years."

"I know." Of course he knew how long it had been. More specifically, it had been nineteen years and three months.

"I'm married."

Flower leis turned to nooses. He held back vomit.

He didn't know that. It was his turn to be silent. He wished she'd look him in the eyes, but she insisted on staring at the sugar packets on the table instead. After a long while, she reached out and gave his hand a tight squeeze. "I'm sorry." She slung her purse over her shoulder, put money down for the bill, and left the café without looking back.

The man sat there, staring at her cold coffee.

ORANGUTAN AND THE WIG
AARON BAILEY

Ingrid sat in her chair, her eyes closed, her mouth moving soundlessly. Allowing herself to relax, she set her mind to focus on the creases and folds of the old armchair. This was her meditation, an exercise of mind over matter. Even as a young child, Ingrid knew she could leave her body. It had been terrifying at first, for her lack of control meant she would float up from her body as her mind hovered between sleep and wakefulness. Weeks of sleepless nights came and went, for she was petrified to lose control. It would be years before she discovered ways to remain anchored to her body or float away when she wished.

Many times in her life, Ingrid sought solace in that quiet place, like when she was bullied at school, during her parents' divorce, their death, and during the passing of her husband, Arthur. In those times, she had flown away to the astral plane. That was the term others had given this other dimension, this other space. Ingrid had learned the term while researching her 'gift', and she understood that others shared her experiences.

Sitting in her chair, she began to feel her body weight fading away. Even though her eyes were closed, Ingrid was able to see. She felt her astral-self float free from flesh and bones. She looked down at her body. The face was pock-marked and liver-spotted. Deep wrinkles made ravines of flesh at the corners of the eyes and mouth. The body was gaunt and haggard, ravaged by time and cancer.

Knowing that she did not have much time to enjoy her flight, Ingrid went to where she always went, the zoo. It had been a haven, much like her flight, from the harshness of life. She would visit whenever she could. Now, unable to walk very far, she only came here as an ethereal apparition. Sometimes animals, and small children, would seem to notice her as she walked around looking at the exhibits. She loved the primates. They amazed her with their similarities to humans. The way they moved, the way they behaved. During this visit, Ingrid spent time with the orangutans in their enclosure.

It was here that something strange occurred. As Ingrid gently stroked one of the orangutans, she felt her astral self merging with the creature's body. She tried frantically to detach herself, to float away, but it was no use, and with a loud pop, she was stuck fast. Then, it dawned upon her. Her body must have died. She had been set adrift in the astral plane and shifted into the nearest 'recipient', that of an orangutan. It was an odd feeling – a different body, a mind other than hers ticking along in the background, as hers floated around, detached.

It took weeks for her to get used to the new arrangement, and with great effort, she could exert a modicum of control of the orangutan. In one such moment, she forced the creature to grasp an exuberant blue wig from the head of a passer-by. She thought that if she was going to be an orangutan, she would look like a lady.

WARSCAPES (2024)
EDWARD BARNFIELD

About three months into the job, Tom Joyce began to dream about the security guard. It was unsettling, because he never usually remembered dreams beyond the standard morning-after anxieties of missed connections or unprepared exams. Now, irrespective of context, the guard was always present when he slept, a constant in the night.

Given that he had spent weeks poring over contemporary visual art – plastic statues in air-conditioned warehouses, digital daubs from up-and-coming South Asian talents – it was almost embarrassing that his subconscious chose to fixate on the tall dark man in the green uniform. He consoled himself that at least these weren't erotic dreams. The guard, while striking, did not spark joy.

Joyce had taken the role of Head of Community Outreach (International) in this remote desert country for prosaic reasons. The Museum, an import from Old Europe, had a prestigious name and ample resources, and the tax-free salary was double what he had earned in London. Besides, his horizons had narrowed back in the city, where the old and the connected kept the best jobs for themselves, and there was always a generation coming up behind you.

Here was a chance to start fresh. Almost everyone in his department seemed to be from somewhere else – a smattering of South Africans, three bright Keralites and two smart young ladies from Kazakhstan. It was a cheerful, open-plan office, with a large Kandinsky on the east wall he had naturally assumed was a print, until his colleagues smirkingly corrected him.

His task was easy enough. The Museum was opening a new display hall as a showcase for the next wave of young artists, to add some spice to the staid old masters and mass-produced masterpieces in the current collection, and he was required to fill it. The only complication seemed to be his ultimate employers.

"You have to understand that our patrons are first and foremost collectors," explained Eris, his manager. "Your job is to enable them to expand their collections. That's what this is all for."

Eris turned out to be an almanac of management aphorisms, honed from a lifetime of project planning in the developing world. Joyce jotted the comment down and then set to work smartening the database and sending out introductory emails to gallerists.

It was only after a few days working with Abdullah, the cheerful intern seconded to his team, that Joyce understood what Eris had meant. Abdullah had soft, babyish hands, smooth to the point of Vaseline, and an obsession with a particular brand of fountain pen. Discussions around culture quickly devolved into analysis of the latest collectors' edition.

"This one has champagne-toned gold fittings," he said, pointing to a photo of a pen on his mobile phone. "It's dedicated to the Great Khan of the Mongol Empire. I'm thinking we could have them in the gift bags."

He was expected to defer to Abdullah on any question of local feeling, despite his youth and apparent fecklessness. As the only national citizen in the office, he was the unofficial representative of the community. Joyce soon found himself recording Abdullah's opinions, too, his spiral-bound notebook bulging with the boy's pseudo-profundities.

"I'm going to America in the summer," he said one lunchtime, "to swim with the sharks. Not in a cage, like. I'm going to actually swim alongside them." Two South Africans at the table, immaculate in matching Prada, exchanged looks.

Yet Abdullah was an essential guide to the Museum and its defining personalities. He knew less than nothing about the art on the walls, but everything about the politics that took place between them.

"Our chairperson is the Sheikha," he confided to Joyce one afternoon. "Her office is the one on the top floor with the bronze door. She doesn't appear often but watch out when she does. That's when decisions get made."

Abdullah was with him when he first saw the guard. They were inspecting the new gallery, the stark white walls still receiving their topcoat, when Joyce noticed a row of backpacks lined up in the lobby. They were the kind designed for toddlers, comfortable straps and primary colours.

"Is there a school trip today?" he asked.

Abdullah giggled. "A visit to an unfinished display hall? Habibi, even our schools aren't that boring. No, it's for the security guards. Their company bought a job lot cheap out of season, and the men use them to carry their lunches."

His comment brought the figures in green into sharper focus, their tatty canvas uniforms and paramilitary berets, standing alert in the empty space. Abdullah kept talking.

"We get the guards cheap out of season, too. Bangladesh, Sudan, Mali. You're lucky if they speak three words of English or Arabic. The company insists on recruiting from all over to prevent cliques from forming."

They paused at the end of the long hall, in the hemispherical vault designed for the largest displays. A high ceiling arched above, and shafts of light caught the walls and floor. The guard was at the far end. He was taller than the others by at least a head, and broad too, a mass of tissue in a tight shirt. He stared straight ahead, not acknowledging their arrival or the streak of sun that danced upon his face, the brow and chin wide as a child's drawing.

"What's his story?" he said.

"The giant? Acromegaly. It's a growth condition. They had to slide two beds together in the labour camp to accommodate him. But he's distinctive."

"He's certainly that."

"Watch out for these men, my friend. Most come from places that don't allow the depiction of the human form. They think it's idolatry, a sin against God. Wait until they find out what this hall is for."

Joyce didn't think much of the encounter at the time. He was busy, consumed with long and short lists, submitting endless proposals to the committee for artists they could invite for the inauguration. They were searching for one candidate for a full show, coupled with an all-expenses residency so that they could create something new and unexpected.

Everybody had their hand out. The galleries in London, who once would have ignored his emails for days, responded with a speed and desperation he hadn't encountered before. The same was true of Tokyo, and Paris, and New York. Something about the combination of high culture and oil money spoke to these people. He'd never been so welcome.

The first time the guard came to him was the night before the final presentation. He'd been working at a frantic pace, long hours, lost weekends. He had narrowed the list down to four candidates: Aurore Olbracht, a young Czech artist who used abstract and figurative artwork inspired by her Moroccan heritage; Mario Sellnik, who mixed images from Instagram with impressionism; and

Xenia Musyoka, who specialised in audio play of sounds from the Masai Mara. Then, at Eris's suggestion, he'd dropped in Atticus Firth-Warwick, a Young British Artist of the 90s. Stale by now, and far from the rich list of his contemporaries, but still a name people recognised. ("It's good to offer a basis for comparison," she said.)

Joyce was proud of the final product. He'd created little graphics showing each artist's 'strategic fit' and 'geographical benefit', with colour coding and pie charts. When he was confident that he'd struck the right balance – nothing too controversial, no one too boring – he moved to the sofa and passed out.

In the dream, he stood alone before the panel. The Sheikha sat at the head on a throne of gold and red velvet. Then there was Eris, severe and unsmiling, and his mother as she was before the cancer. And then there was the fourth panellist, in a purple suit with matching tie – the guard, the chair creaking beneath his weight. He was holding something, a polaroid photo of a family, and the sight of it filled Joyce with this overwhelming sense of sadness. He tried to speak, but his mouth was stuffed with wet tissue, the drip at the back of his throat making him gag. Then he woke.

When he arrived next morning, Eris was waiting by his desk.

"Let's talk," she said.

The meeting was cancelled. There would be no need for the presentation. The Sheikha, on one of her regular trips to Europe, had discovered an up-and-coming artist all by herself. He would be arriving on Thursday, and Joyce was to chaperone him ahead of the show.

"I did tell you they were collectors," Eris said. "Abdullah collects pens, and Her Excellency collects people."

The chosen creator was Ayman Adnan. The Sheikha was impressed with the minor storm he had conjured at one of the smaller biennials. His work, 'Warscapes', used photography from global skirmishes and superimposed animated imagery over them, so that a smoking bombsite in Former Yugoslavia became a swimming hole for cartoon ducks. People agonised over the appropriateness of the concept and noted that Adnan rarely credited the original photographers, some of whom had subsequently died in other conflicts. It was the kind of controversary you could comfortably take a side on. Joyce had ruled him out in the first cut of the longlist.

The artist came off the plane complaining, unhappy with the air conditioning and the quality of his welcome. The Sheikha had promised unlimited resources, he said, but his flight hadn't even been first class. A little man, goatish, with a reek of old leather and cheap cigarettes, his grey hair pulled back in a tight ponytail. They had to change his hotel three times and recruit the two new quite disreputable suppliers he insisted upon. His inauguration project was as basic as it was lazy – he was going to work on four huge canvases of contemporary urban sieges with a hand-picked team of college students. (Eris remarked that he was effectively outsourcing production, but she said it quietly away from upper management ears).

Fortunately, Abdullah stepped up and shouldered most of the burden. He formed an odd bond with Adnan, spending hours leafing through catalogues of designer pens with him. Tom Joyce spent most of his time apologising on behalf of their guest, who left unpaid bills at boutiques and restaurants across the capital.

The guard become more prominent in his dreams. He sat, stoic, on the train journeys and wedding parties of his youth, his presence taunting him, or stood behind the desk of a funeral parlour, staring ahead as always. Sometimes he carried the photograph, and sometimes he dropped it on the floor of a dirty carriage or deep in the wet grass. Joyce woke more exhausted than before.

There was a VIP inspection one day ahead of opening. The Sheikha arrived, the Board trailing behind her like ducklings, and the whole team was lined up in the lobby to greet them. Abdullah was designated as the guide, relegating Joyce to the menial duty of ensuring the tetraptych was hung straight.

Standing there, watching the stately waddle of Her Excellency as she viewed the artwork, it was hard for Joyce not to feel the weight of all that futility. He looked hard at the canvases, tried to find meaning in the burned-out buildings and anime-style graphics, but could see nothing. Then he heard a voice behind him.

"Mullivaikkal," it said, strangely whispered and high-pitched.

Joyce turned and saw the figure from his dream, closer than he'd been before, pointing at the third canvas of the set. The photo was a hospital of some kind, in a tropical-looking location. There had been heavy shelling, and there were bodies in the background, which the cartoon graffiti turned into sunbathers.

In all the time they had dissected and discussed this project, it hadn't occurred to them that the photos might include a massacre someone recognised, or worse, had a connection to. That it might be this man, the tall Sri Lankan Tamil with the growth disorder who had haunted Tom for so long, seemed almost impossibly unlucky. There was a flurry as his colleagues moved the giant to another corner.

After that, the rehearsal came and went. The Sheikha was pleased, and Ayman Adnan stopped complaining when he received his first payment, and everyone felt the thin buzz of professional satisfaction. A cadre of tame media toured the exhibition and gave it rave reviews, and the opening party happened, and all was right with the world.

A few weeks later, Joyce woke with an anaesthetised sensation. His phone had been ringing for some time and it took a moment to realise why he had slept so deeply. It had been the first night in months that he hadn't encountered the guard. The future stretched out before him, no more counting the time until opening day, no more babysitting bad-tempered artists.

When he arrived at the office, police cars were parked outside the hall, along with a fire engine. Someone had entered the building at around midnight and set light to the third of the four large canvases, leaving only embers and scorch.

Investigators were on the scene already, questioning the staff. Tom Joyce sat at his desk and waited to be called, a fist of tension tightening in his stomach. He knew the culprit, and the motive. He also knew his time in this place was over. Someone would need to be blamed, after all, and as the outsider and organiser of the inaugural display, he'd be the ideal scapegoat.

The man in his dream had been trying to tell him for so long.

ON THIN ICE
JANE BRADLEY

She is much smaller than he remembers. That had always surprised him, when he hadn't seen her for a while, just how tiny she actually was.

On the ice, she flew weightlessly above his head, spinning like a dervish, the skirt of her costume fluttering through the air as he reached up to catch her, looking up to her. Always looking up.

Then when they were done, standing on solid ground again as they waited for their scores, it felt like she towered over everyone else on her steely blades.

It was her personality too. She dominated every room, every conversation, on or off her skates. Now, for once, she is not glittering, not sparkling as she does on television, her bright lipstick contrasting against her brilliant white teeth. She is – and he had never thought this was possible – subdued, almost bowed.

"Vincent."

Her voice is low. He doesn't say anything at first, just

fixes his eyes on the grey tweed cushion of the chair behind her, avoiding her piercing gaze. Of course she would have chosen a place like this for them to meet. He's lived in this town for fifteen years and never walked through the revolving door into this bastion of luxury. She flies in for ten minutes and already knows the best places in town.

He wonders if she's staying here, has checked herself into one of the suites upstairs. He pictures the contents of her overnight bag strewn across the bed… the silk underwear, the Dior make-up.

She stands to greet him, half up, half down as if she doesn't know where her body should be. Then she straightens and lifts her arms slightly, into a *demi bras* position – he notes she is still physically graceful even in awkward social situations – and lowers them to her side again. He catches a waft of her perfume. Chanel Number 5. It had always seemed so exotic, so sophisticated before. Now it whiffs of cliché.

She gestures theatrically to the seat next to her, inclines her head on one side.

"Please."

He is irritated to notice that she is still using these affected French mannerisms, despite her indisputable origins in the London commuter belt.

"What do you want? What is this about?" He sounds aggressive, but he doesn't care. He hasn't thought about what to say to her, how he would react when he saw her.

He almost didn't come.

She sighs.

"Will you sit, please? Just for five minutes."

Her tone is beseeching, her lashes lowered against her smooth cheeks. His heart starts to race and his palms are clammy, but he remains standing, focusing on pushing his shoulders back, perfectly aligning his spine. *Straight and tall, Vincent, straight and tall.* That's what their ballet coach used to say.

It's a power game between them. If he gives in, he knows he's lost, even though he's not sure yet what the game is. He shakes his head, firmly, briefly enjoying this advantage, however small.

"Vincent, I'm broke."

That's the last thing he expects her to say. He sits.

"Broke? But…" He waves an arm around the room, at the lavish bar-restaurant where the business trip bankers are sipping their pre-dinner cocktails.

She shrugs.

"I didn't know where else to suggest. I've been here once before – did you know that? And this is where I stayed. It's nice."

Of course he knew that she'd been here before. He'd seen the posters when they'd gone up around town – "*with guest judge Amanda Gray*" – and quickly booked himself some leave, spending her three-day tour date in a damp cottage in the Lake District.

"Why did you come, Amanda?"

She winces at his directness.

"I need you, Vincent."

He would have killed to hear those words fifteen years ago… they would have thrilled him. But now, he just feels annoyed.

She is picking at a loose thread on the cuff of her cream blouse.

"They want me to do a tour. They want me to skate."

"Skate?" She hasn't skated in almost a decade, as far as he knows. Not since she won the gold at Vancouver. She's a media darling now. She's on all of the TV shows, the skating one, even the dancing one – always as a judge, not a coach – but he never saw her step onto the ice. He knows, he's watched them all.

"My agent has pitched it to one of the big operators. A comeback tour." She laughs. "Not competition, of course, not at my age. But she thinks people would pay to see me skate again."

"And can you? Skate, I mean?"

She glares at him, but she knows the question is a fair one.

She's never been a solo skater. She's more of a dancer, who isn't bad on a set of blades. She has the artistic talent, the gymnastic figure – though looking at her now, her body has got softer, still skinny, but less muscular – but she was never an athlete. She can't jump, she couldn't land a double axel even in her prime.

"I can't skate on my own, of course I can't. But I could with you."

Vincent, who has been holding his breath, exhales. She wants to ice dance again, she needs a partner.

"What about Joe?"

Olympic gold medallist Joe, who'd stepped neatly into his shoes after they split – in more ways than one. Who had partnered Amanda to the top of her career as he, Vincent, had watched on the fuzzy television set in the rink staff room, surrounded by peeling paint and blunt hire skates.

She lowers her voice.

"Joseph is an alcoholic. He weighs 120 kilos. He couldn't stand up on a pair of skates if his life depended on it, these days. Anyway, we're not exactly on the best of terms, not after the divorce. I need *you*, Vincent."

She pauses. "And besides, you're still a skater."

He thinks about the skating he'd done that day, before he'd crossed the city to meet her. Forward glides, two-foot turns and snow plough stops. Until an elderly man called Bob had fallen and hit his head, putting an abrupt end to the class.

He wonders if she realises that he hasn't performed a proper routine since the last time they skated together. The World Figure Skating Championships in Dortmund in 2004, when they'd come a respectable fourth. He'd thought it was respectable, at any rate. She'd thrown down the bouquet their coach had given her onto the rubber mat at the side of the rink and stormed off before the scores had even come in, screaming at him in front of the other competitors, in earshot of the crowds – and the TV cameras.

"You're incompetent, stupid!" she'd raged. "A child

could have performed that final set of twizzles better than you."

The faces around the rink were pitying. His cheeks were burning with shame as he sat in the kiss and cry corner on his own, waiting for the scores, the empty space next to him on the sofa evidence of his failure.

She'd arrived back in their hotel room seven hours later, crying and repentant, her make-up smeared down her face.

It was then that she'd told him her wonderful news and he had believed things might be different between them. That they had a chance of a happy future together, a very different future. When she'd fallen asleep, exhausted, he had stayed awake for hours, watching her perfect face in the moonlight, nestled against the white pillow as she breathed softly.

That was three weeks before he left.

They sit. She doesn't fiddle with her rings, he stares at a dark spot on the otherwise pristine carpet. Neither of them speak. He is too stunned to respond, she is waiting for an answer.

Suddenly a woman is by their table, her round cheeks flushed pink, one hand pushing back her frizzy, highlighted hair from her face.

"Amanda Gray? It is, isn't it? I said to my husband it looked like you, but he said it couldn't be, you look so much smaller than you do on television, but then everyone does, don't they?"

As Amanda automatically turns on the charm,

responds to the woman's request for photos, autographs, video messages for her daughter, Vincent gets up and walks away. He's barely made it through the revolving doors, past the suited concierge, when he hears her heels clattering on the pavement behind him.

"Wait, Vincent, I'm so sorry."

He's never heard her say that word before. *Sorry.*

"I'm sorry that silly woman came along, just as we were starting to have a proper chat." She is smiling at him now in exactly the same way she'd smiled at the fan, her perfectly manicured nails laid on his arm.

"If we could just talk about some of the details, it'll be a wonderful opportunity, for both of us, I mean."

He shakes his head. "The answer is no, Amanda. Absolutely not. Never."

Her face falls. She isn't used to being told no, he knows that.

"What? Are you crazy? Just think about it. The publicity, the money..."

A bus pulls up outside of the hotel. He has no idea what number it is, or where it is going, but jumps on board anyway, scrabbling in his pocket for change.

As it drives away, he can hear her voice through the open window. "Vincent, no, don't be like that, just imagine..."

He slumps into the bus seat. His hands are shaking. What Amanda is suggesting sounds unreal. Of course he isn't going to do it. He closes his eyes, suddenly exhausted.

When he looks up, he realises his fears were right. This bus isn't going anywhere near his flat. It is pouring with rain as he gets off, finding himself in an unfamiliar suburb. Even the kebab shop is closed, its graffitied metal shutters pulled over a poky window.

He's left his coat in the hotel, with his wallet in the pocket. The loose change in his jeans has dwindled to a couple of 10ps and a 20p. Not enough to catch another bus.

Thank god his neighbour has a key. He's getting soaked as he trudges home, three miles through parts of the city visitors never see, but he doesn't care.

As he turns the corner into his street, a car flashes past, drenching him as it speeds through a puddle. He opens the door to his stairwell to find someone sitting in the darkness on the bottom step. She is clutching a dark bundle to her chest.

"You forgot your coat."

She holds it out for him to take. She is soaked too, her blonde hair plastered to her head. "Your driving licence was in your pocket, so I knew where to come. Well, actually, the taxi dropped me off in the wrong place, so I had to walk the last part. I've been waiting for you for ages."

There is a tone of petulance in her voice and he almost finds himself apologising, but stops just in time. Force of habit. He takes the coat, finds his keys in the pocket and starts to climb past her, up the stairs to his front door.

"Thanks for bringing it back."

He turns away, putting the key in the lock.

"Thanks? Is that all? Aren't you going to invite me in?"

The last thing he wants is Amanda in his flat. It has been fifteen years since they were last alone in a room together.

"No." He has to stand firm.

He pauses, knowing he sounds dramatic, but that's what she responds to.

"Goodbye, Amanda."

"I'm not leaving."

The petulant tone is back.

"What?"

"I'll stay here until you agree to talk to me. I'll sleep on the stairs if I have to."

She looks so out of place, sitting there in the dingy stairwell, in her designer, beige mac and suede, heeled boots. She stretches out on the lower step. He tries to avert his gaze from her long, slim legs in their expensive skinny jeans.

"It's quite comfortable."

Her eyes are sparkling now. She is actually enjoying this.

Vincent shrugs.

"Suit yourself."

Inside, he switches on the TV, but he can't relax. She's there, on the other side of the door. So close he can almost touch her.

He makes dinner, quickly whipping up an omelette from some eggs and leftover mushrooms in the fridge. She is singing now, to entertain herself or to irritate him, he's not sure. If he puts his ear to the door, he can make out the words…

Phil Collins. Great. It's 10.30pm. The neighbours are going to go crazy if she keeps this up.

He cracks.

"For God's sake, Amanda, come inside, then. Just shut up."

He grabs her arm and pulls her through the door. Her smile is triumphant. Dammit.

He moves towards the kitchen. His flat is little more than a bedsit, the kitchen is a row of cupboards and a stove at the back of the living room. He is faintly embarrassed for her to see him living like this, then he remembers that she's in an even worse position, despite outward appearances.

"Coffee?"

He has a feeling it's going to be a long night.

She sinks into the sofa and takes a sip. "You always did make great coffee, Vincent. Great food, generally. I've never eaten as well as I did when I lived with you."

She sniffs theatrically. She can smell the omelette. Tough, he's not going to make her one, however much she drops hints. He thinks of the *coq au vin* he'd cooked for her the night he'd left, when his world had fallen to pieces, but the stew had just continued to calmly bubble on the stove. He wonders what happened to it after he went, if she'd sat down on her own just as calmly and eaten it anyway.

He's tempted to ask, but he doesn't. He's not sure he wants to know. He perches on a wooden stool he usually uses as a coffee table, positioning himself as far away from the sofa as possible.

"Say your piece and then leave, would you? It's late and I've got to work tomorrow."

She tucks her feet elegantly under her, settling in for the long haul.

"It's your opportunity to show everyone what you can do, Vincent. People don't often get a second chance: this is yours. There'd be no rules, no restrictions, you can do what you like."

Vincent can still land some triple jumps, not that he'd had to since he switched to ice dancing more than two decades ago. Sometimes, after everyone else had left the rink – once he's finished teaching the Jennifers and Bobs how to chassé on a circle – he sneaks back inside, flicks on the huge light switches and skates for the sake of skating, testing himself to see what he can still do.

"You should have been the star back then, not me."

She's just trying it on now.

"Don't lay it on so thick, Amanda. I'm not going to fall for your bullshit, not anymore."

"I'm not. I mean it. You were the real skater. I couldn't believe it when you agreed to partner me."

She's pulling paperwork out of her bag, a thick sheaf of sheets dotted with fluorescent tabs.

"This is the contract. Just take a look."

He is about to push it away, when he sees the number. She has highlighted it in yellow marker, as if she knew he'd miss it otherwise.

"Jesus."

Her eyes are sparkling and her lips are pressed together like a child waiting to give someone a present.

That amount of money would change his life. He could move out of this poky little flat, get himself somewhere decent, somewhere a man of his age should live. Maybe move abroad to look for another job, at a better rink.

He hands it back to her.

"No. It's not worth it."

"Vincent!"

She's crushed, she obviously thought she had him.

"I'm not talking about this anymore. Just go, will you?"

"Go?" She bites her lip. "The problem is, I don't have anywhere to go. I was meant to be on the last train back to London and now… obviously, I'm not. Would you mind if I stay here? On the sofa, of course. I'll leave first thing, as soon as there's a train, you'll never even hear me go."

He sighs.

"It doesn't sound like I have much choice."

Half an hour later, he's tossing and turning on the lumpy sofa. He regrets insisting that Amanda had the bed. He won't make that mistake again.

At 5am, he gives up trying to sleep. He opens a drawer and takes out a small box. He opens it and turns one of the medals over in his palm, briefly admiring the engraving on the back: a figure skater with her leg held high in the air in a Bielmann spiral.

They had been so happy, he remembers, recalling the applause from the crowds as they finished their skate, the sheer jubilation as their scores were announced and the feel of her hand in his – nervous and trembling –

as they stood at the top of the podium for the first time. European Champions 2003.

He makes a pot of coffee on the stove and takes two mugs into the dark bedroom. When he opens the door, a shaft of light falls onto Amanda's sleeping face and he is transported back to that night in Dortmund.

He switches on the light and feels a glimmer of satisfaction as she is shocked out of sleep. She sits up, blinking confusedly at him.

"What is it? What's going on?"

He hands her one of the mugs.

"Okay. I'm in. What do we have to do?"

SPACE AND TIME
CHRIS BROCK

It had been a long time since I'd really stopped and thought back to those days. The years passed. The anniversaries came and went. But ultimately, all it took was that one chance comment in a conversation the other day… and suddenly it all hit home.

It had felt like a time of great progress. The wireless was full of talk of Concorde, robots, artificial hearts… But this was the *real* biggie – Man was going to the moon.

Dad bought us our first television set, in anticipation. "It's only black and white," he warned me, as though I might have thought that we were suddenly made of money. It stood there, proudly in the corner of the sitting room, from where a man called Percy pontificated on how to re-design your garden.

"You promise you'll wake me up for the moonwalk?" I pleaded once again, keen to reinforce a pledge already made.

"Yes, son," dad said. And he meant it.

Although mam must have given him one of her looks, because he sighed heavily. "Doris," he said, "just think – for a million years, man has gazed up at the moon – he has wondered and he has dreamed. Now, finally, he is going there – and we get the chance to witness it…!"

She couldn't argue with that one, so instead, she smiled indulgently, leant over, and kissed him.

Everything seemed set.

•

It was only about twenty-four hours later, though, as we sat up for tea, that life suddenly stopped being quite so straightforward. As mam began serving the mashed potato, dad walked in and sat down. And, without looking up, she said, "I've just had my mam on the phone…" Her voice was really weird – I had never heard it like that before – and when I looked at her, I could see that she had been crying. "It's Archie…" she said.

Dad looked at up her. And he mouthed something.

And mam nodded, her hands over her face.

Dad put his fork down. "Bloody Hell!" he said.

Suddenly, mam wailed, "It's been two years, Bernard – we knew he was very ill."

"Is it that long?" he asked, sheepishly. And he reached out across the table and he took her hand.

I, meanwhile, sat there in silence. Waiting guiltily for the mashed potato that never came. I knew of Uncle Archie, of course – mam had told me they'd been really close as kids – thick as thieves, she'd say, wistfully. And I must have met him a few times, too – though obviously not for a couple of years. So I felt pretty bad now that I could scarcely even picture the man, let alone muster any feelings of sadness.

•

The plans were soon made: mam and dad were travelling to Grandma's for the funeral on the 20th, and I was to be packed off to my friend Ian's house.

"So we're not going to watch the moon landings together?" I asked.

And dad looked down at the carpet.

"But you promised," I wailed.

"I'm really sorry," he mumbled.

"Will Ian's dad wake me up for the moonwalk?" I asked.

And mam cut in with an exasperated, "I don't know, dear." And I knew well enough then not to push it.

"I know it's unfortunate," dad said, trying to be conciliatory, "but you need to be brave and strong for your mother. Okay?"

"Okay," I said. Because that was what I had to say. But all I wanted to do, desperately, was to burst into tears.

•

When I got delivered to Ian's house, his mam looked me over. "Are you alright?" she asked me.

It took a moment to work out what she meant, but then it twigged – and I gave her my best 'it's sad, but I'm bearing up' kind of a face.

And she grabbed me, and hugged me hard into her apron.

Ian padded over.

"Hi, Ian," I said. Freeing myself from Mrs Patterson.

"Hi."

And before he could distract me, I set about scoping the place out.

"There's no TV," I declared after a good nosey.

"No," he said.

"But you used to have one!"

"Yes," he nodded. "But it broke a while back, and dad decided not to get a new one. He says they're just not worth it."

"Are you joking?"

"No."

"But the moonwalk... Aren't you going to watch it?"

He looked confused. "But that's in the middle of the night, isn't it?"

That hit me such a blow – but still, I was hardly about to give up now. There *had* to be some way...

Just then, Ian's dad waddled in. He had been working out the back, concreting a new patio or something, and he was all dusty and bothered. "Oh," he said, when he saw me. And that was the extent of his interest. A miserable man at the best of times, he had clearly forgotten that I was coming. I'd be wasting my time working on him.

Upstairs, with Ian and his little sister Kathleen, we tried being astronauts – but my heart wasn't in it. I began rummaging through their toy box. Suddenly, I struck gold. "Ian," I said excitedly, "what's this?"

"It's my telescope," he said.

"Does it work, though?"

He frowned. "Well, it makes things look bigger –if that's what you mean?"

"Then we've got it!" I declared. "We've actually got it!"

They both looked at me, none the wiser.

"This telescope," I said, "is made for looking at the heavens."

"Where your uncle's gone?" Kathleen asked.

"We can point it at the moon…"

Ian saw where I was going with this. "And see the moonwalk?" he asked, his face sceptical. "I don't think it's that good."

"Well, we might not see *them*," I conceded. "But we might see Apollo 11… or see something!"

"Like when I saw Santa Claus?" Kathleen asked.

Thing was, though, their room was at one end of the house. And its one, small window basically faced straight onto next-door's brickwork. "Do you think we could take it out into the garden?" I asked.

"In the middle of the night?" Ian asked, incredulous. "No way. Mam and dad would have a fit."

"What if we wait until your parents are asleep, and then we just sneak downstairs and do it in secret?"

Silence.

"And if they catch us?" Ian asked eventually.

"Yeah…?"

"They'd kill us!" said Ian. "They'd literally kill us."

I looked up, startled, and Kathleen, sat cross-legged on her bunk bed, was nodding vigorously. "Literally," she insisted.

"It's worth the risk, though. Isn't it?" I asked. I said it without thinking. Certain, I'm sure, that Ian would say no. But the longer he sat there, not saying no… the more nervous I became.

At last he raised his head. "Alright," he said, a strange smile slowly spreading across his face, "let's do it!"

So, we had our mission – there was no backing out now.

•

I awoke to darkness. A different bed. Distant breathing. Otherness. Slowly disentangling the memories from my dreaming, I found Uncle Archie, the telescope, and the waiting moon. I remembered the eternal wait for Mr and Mrs Patterson to finally climb the stairs and go to bed. For our adventure to begin…

"Ian?" I called out softly, speculatively. "Ian?"

In her bunk bed, Kathleen stirred. "What?" she groaned.

"I was calling Ian," I whispered.

"I know," she said, sounding like she was stretching. "But I'm coming too."

•

It's a weird thing, creeping around a house at night time, blind, though your eyes are open, hands out in front of you, feeling, searching. Feet taking little, shuffling steps, uncertain what they might crash into. Weirder still, though, when it's not your house you're creeping around in! I found the wall; inched along it until reached the door handle, pulled…

Behind me, Ian snorted. "That's the cupboard, silly," he giggled.

I felt my face burning. "Alright then," I whispered, "you go first."

Out on the landing, we could hear the slow, low snoring of Mr Patterson. And – shot through with this queer, electric thrill, this astonishment at our own daring – we began creeping down the stairs.

Holding on to each other as we went. Down and slowly down. Stepping out each time into nothingness.

Every little noise seemed to amplify so wildly.

Creak followed agonising creak. As we knew that at any moment we might awaken the dreadful wrath of Mr or Mrs Patterson.

As I wondered how it was that we hadn't woken them already.

"Shh!"

"You shush!"

"It wasn't me!"

"Well, it wasn't me!"

"Will you just stop pushing back there?"

On we went. Down and slowly down.

Until at long, long last, we made it to the hallway.

An open door, a shaft of light from a poorly shut curtain, and suddenly, we could see where we were going.

A noise. A shadow shifting.

"He-llo there! He-llo there!" said Ian in a silly voice. As the dog snuffled, and wagged its tail, slapping it hard against my legs. "We need to be really quiet," Ian told her – rather too loudly.

"Here, doggy," called Kathleen, "here, doggy."

I made straight for the back door – it was locked.

"Where's the key?" I asked.

Ian shrugged. "Dunno," he said. "Is it not in the door?"

"Well, no – or I wouldn't have asked you!"

We scoured the room, the shelves and pots and table-tops, but it was nowhere to be seen.

Frustrated, I wandered over to the window. We were so close!

And then I blinked – I actually blinked in disbelief at what my eyes were seeing. Because out there, where their garden should have been, there was instead another world – a strange and lumpen desert of mounds and hollows.

A queer, silver light shone down in dappled shafts, illuminating patches and casting long, black shadows. Everything was still, and quite eerie.

Ian came and stood on a chair next to me. He opened

the window, and the cool and clean night air came drifting in.

"Can you get out that way?" I managed, still wondering whether I was dreaming.

"I think so," he said, apparently unconcerned by the craterous alien world that had supplanted his garden. "You want to try?"

The window was small, and rather high up. "You try," I suggested. "You're taller than me."

"Exactly," he said. "*I* might get stuck." Looking thoughtful, he stepped back down and disappeared.

Suddenly, he was back, with the soft, licking mass of dog in his arms.

I stared.

"What are you doing?" Kathleen demanded.

He lifted the whimpering creature up higher and higher and – before either of us could react – dumped her straight out through the open window.

There was a great, heavy thump. And a startled, yelping whine. Then she was off, diving away into the shadows.

"What d'you do that for?" Kathleen demanded.

"To see if it was possible," said Ian.

"And?" I asked.

"Well, she got out alright."

"You dropped her!" cried Kathleen.

"She'll be fine," Ian insisted. "They've got nine lives, haven't they?"

"How are we going to get her back in again?" I asked.

"She'll just have to stay out there."

"No-o-o-o!" Kathleen wailed alarmingly. "What if she never comes back? What if she's just running round and round the town forever and ever?"

Ian ignored her. "I'm going to give it a try!" he declared. And suddenly he was up and swinging first one leg, then his whole body through. He landed with a great clomp, and then a skip.

"You okay?"

"Yeah!" he said, breathless, excited. "You coming?"

"Sure…"

"Careful, though, there's a step here."

"A big one?"

"Mmm," said Ian, mulling this over. "Not so big… more… kind of medium-sized."

So, I hoisted myself up. Swung myself through, and suddenly I, too, was out, and walking in this fantastical, silver-lit world.

"What about me?" Kathleen asked through the window. "How can I get out?"

Ian and I looked at each other.

"You'll have to stay there," Ian said. "We'll need you to help us get back in again."

"But… I want to see…!"

Suddenly, I was inspired. "Kathleen," I said, "you're our Command Module Pilot, our Michael Collins. It's the most important job of all."

"Really?" she asked, brightening a little.

"Definitely! Oh, and Kathleen?"

"Yes?"

"Pass us the telescope out, will you?"

•

Slowly, cautiously, Ian and I made our way out and amongst the strange, sandy-looking mounds, our slippers raising a fine, grey, powdery dust as we went.

"What's that?" I asked of the large object in front of us?

"It's mam's washing-line," Ian said. "It's fallen over. Here…"

And together we re-planted it, one solitary tea-towel – with its silhouetted scenes of 'The Yorkshire Dales' – hanging there like a banner.

The moon hung huge and serene above us. Ian pointed the telescope.

"What can you see?" I asked impatiently.

"Well, I've got it alright," he said, "but it's still quite small. I think they're probably just a bit too far away."

Kathleen called out to us, "Guys, what can you see out there? You're taking ages."

"We'll not be long," Ian call-whispered back.

We dragged a couple of deck chairs out from the shed, and we sat there. Amongst the upturned wheelbarrows, the abandoned buckets and shovels. Staring up at the heavens, the endless canopy above us.

"It's amazing, isn't it?"

"Mmm," I said. And I saw that his face was illuminated.

"It's just so-o-o-o big. And we're… s-o-o-o small! I never realised!"

"Do you reckon my Uncle Archie really is up there?" I asked.

Ian pulled a face. "I thought that they were burying him in the ground?" he said.

"Yeah," I said, my brain no clearer.

There was a thump. A strange metallic clattering. Then Kathleen came pattering over.

"What are you doing out here? You've abandoned your–"

"Pah," she interrupted, "you were taking ages. Anyway, I brought you these…" and she held up a large biscuit tin.

"Great!" said Ian.

"Provisions," I said, helping myself to one of Mrs Patterson's ginger biscuits. "Er… good call!"

Kathleen dragged herself a little fold-up chair over, and she sat down beside us. "Wow!" she said.

"I know," said Ian.

Kathleen took the telescope from him and she pointed it up at the moon. "Where are they then?" she asked.

"Too far away," I said.

"Just think," said Ian. "All these stars and moons and planets and galaxies… This moon landing – it's just the beginning, isn't it? Next it'll be Mars, Jupiter, all the other ones. Perhaps when we're grown ups…"

"I think I'd like to be an astronaut," Kathleen said.

"Yeah?" I imagined her hurtling through space in a tiny rocket of her own.

"Definitely," she nodded, gazing heavenwards, chewing thoughtfully. "Either that or a hairdresser."

•

Who knows how long we sat there? Eyes full of the sky-scape, and wide with such possibilities that we had never imagined before. Our mouths full of biscuit. Shivering in just our pyjamas and our slippers. The clouds came and went. The stars twinkled... disappeared... and returned. As the fat, cratered moon, with its unseen visitors, slid its way slowly across the sky. And we sat there in that strange and alien light. Wondering. Dreaming...

Eventually, it was Ian who called time on it all. "One last look," he suggested. "We're all turning blue here."

Kathleen passed me the telescope and I peered up at the rather blurry moon.

"Still nothing?" Ian asked.

"Nah," I said, handing it on to him.

"Nothing," he confirmed. "Must be on their tea break or something."

So, giggling and shivering, we stuffed our chairs back into the shed, and we hurried over to the house. And with the odd, last wistful look behind us, we helped each other back in through the window.

And before we knew it, we were back in our beds again, snug and cosy and beaming wildly, as though we had all just shared the craziest dream imaginable, as if we had each been touched by magic.

•

Of course, we could scarcely imagine what had really been going on up there. I had to wait till the following evening, back home, to see those recorded images of Neil Armstrong and Buzz Aldrin bouncing around in their spacesuits and all of that. But then again, as they were busy up there, I bet that they could scarcely have conceived of the three of us, and of our own particular mission to a small back garden in northern England. And it's nice to think that – in a funny sort of way – that kind of makes us even.

For the best part of ten years after that night, I would visit Ian and Kathleen's now and again. We had other adventures too, of course, but there was never to be another one quite like it. We were all growing up, and somehow we were slowly drifting apart. Eventually, Ian and I both left for university and, when her time came, I think Kathleen probably did too. And I never saw either of them again.

I have no idea where Kathleen is now, or whether she ever made it to become an astronaut. Or a hairdresser. And for many, many years, I knew nothing of Ian either. Then, in that chance comment in a conversation just the other day, I discovered that he had died. It was a few years back, it seems – and I don't know any more about it than that.

Looking up at the heavens now, I see that same impassive moon. I see the same bright shining stars that we were once all held so rapt by, and I wonder. I wonder if Ian is up there now with my Uncle Archie – and with the oh-so-many others who have left us with the passing of the years?

Whatever the truth of it, though, I like to think that in that small suburban garden, one legacy of our moonlit mission still remains: three small-ish sets of footprints – forever impressed into Mr Patterson's slow-drying cement work.

THE CREATOR
CATHY BRYANT

I had created the perfect creature: the Cat. I still had an awful lot to do, but I knew that nothing could top that feline. My goal now was to provide the perfect servant for the cat.

It might seem old-fashioned to you, but believe me (and you ought to, when you consider whose team I'm on), it was futuristic as anything when I did it: I drew up my plans on paper. Naturally I didn't *need* to, but I like fun as much as the next deity's assistant.

I had Humans just about half-done (opposable thumbs so they could get food for cats, intelligence so that they could deduce how best to serve cats, and so on) when it happened. Soup, a graceful tabby, and Bang, a cheeky black-and-white moggy, wandered in, jumped up, sat on the plans and began a leisurely wash.

I know. I could have made them want to get off, with the merest wave of my wing and exercise of my powers.

But I'd given cats completely free will. After all, they were perfect. Why shouldn't they do what they liked?

It would have felt terribly rude to disturb them, too. A cat wash is a gentle, rhythmic ritual. I'd as soon throw the planets out of their courses as disturb a cat at her ablutions.

You'll tell me that I didn't need the plans. If I wished, I could see through the plans, or make them manifest elsewhere. If I wished… but I didn't. There was just something so aesthetically and *spiritually* pleasing about the cats and their washing (and then their sleeping). I was on a deadline with Humans, but I didn't care. Sometimes you have to stop what you're doing and watch a cat have a wash.

Well, you know the rest. I put Humans through as they were. A disaster. They were clever without being wise, functional without being responsible, and they even forgot why they were made.

"What is the meaning of life?" they ask. "Why are we here?"

To serve cats, you fools! Now go and do a better job of it! And never, ever, ever disturb a cat who is sleeping or washing – unless the future of the world is at stake.

As for me, I was fired from my job and stripped of my powers. Oh, they were kind – I have a little place of my own, and a garden, and enough to eat. There I sit and remember, and try not to cry all the time.

And then Soup and Bang will jump on my lap to be stroked and massaged. And when they start purring, I'm as happy, fulfilled and godlike as anyone or anything in the whole of creation.

TAPESTRY

TIMOTHY BURTON-MARTIN

"Yarm was. Stockton is. Middlesbrough will be."
An old proverb

Pencils scratch on the page.

We start with the farm. Twenty-five people grasp and yank at the soil, dripping clothes trickle and feed the earth they toil over. Others pull shire mares and mules over cleared ground, kicking rusted helmets. Workers hover by the fresh ground and fill in the lines with a seed that sprouts wings and skims the soil, tethered to its roots. They sew lines in their lives, over the tapestry from before. Buttercups and Queen Anne's lace cover the ground behind the forest of hawthorns, ancient coins buried in their roots.

A carriage from a few towns away pulls up. Workers buzz from field to orchard to pasture and ignore the strange men in dark suits and neckties. They leave. Green tethers swell while workers restitch off white clothes with yellow patches that smell of parsley and polish. Once again, the carriage arrives, suits hand paper to the workers. They stop and look around at fading hawthorns, buttercups grow in between wooden houses. Gather potatoes around budding brick trees, eyes up in uniformed rows.

Workers go from field to pasture and file into piled stone cairns, buried halfway in the ground. From seed, growth begins. Pencil marks etch what was.

Click, snap.

Ships strangled with twine skim past docks along the river, wood covered tin fills up hawthorn and oak barges. Wings of cloth open and fly from Mine to Parish to Cathedral, tethered by the string of water that runs into the globule sea. They always return to the docks where buttercups huddle around surviving Hawthorne. Sailors watch workers file into black belching chimneys and butcher shops in a square, smelling of smoke and polish.

Children send hoops flying down streets that have taken root and sprout new streets. By the end of the road, the children file to build new factories and butcher shops. The hoop rolls by itself.

Workers huddle around scaffolding that grows bricks and mortar and sprout hanging arches and carved figures. They sew dark stone while yellow skies flow to ocean grey. Finally, the solid stem flowers into brass bells under a white face, their peal echoes like scattered petals.

Spinning jennies stitch time into dresses, sewn in lines along the grey stone walls of the factory. Women rub black patches into rough clothes and wait in lines behind the doubling machines. All sit on command and rattle away time. Line, click, change, click. Thread crosses over itself. They leave on a line when steam bellows in the yellowed sky.

The chimneys eat their fill and send iron children running on hoops down iron roads and devour coal poured from ships. Little chimneys belch out steam as they screech to the lapping sea before coming home. Men file into carriages and are pulled along from the end of the road. When they arrive, streets shift and cross each other into bridges that lift like metal wings. New books, new houses, new lives. A suit under a blanket crouches behind a metal eye and stares at the world. Hands shift, necks nudge, breaths held in a pose for the camera.

Click-flash! Lenses blink and it all changes, eyes stare at the liquid concrete pouring into an unending mould. A moment snapped from what is and frozen, waiting to move.

Cranks scratch metal eyes that watch the click of a hulking metal beast pull itself across the river. A man falls down and snaps his hat. Men grasp and yank him back up to their side that was left behind, while the others fade out of frame. All look ahead at what will be.

Buttercups grow around broken glass, faded stone arches. Silent bells toll the time, their peal echoes down set concrete and plastic windows. Statues fade under an ocean of blue ink, faded names overlap. Ancient coins melt into stone floors. Old pictures written on the wall with pencil marks: This is what we were.

Workers file their own way down the railroad that ends at the ocean. Children skate down the road, under the train bridge to the other half. Glowing screens fill the shadows, a world behind the world sewing us together reveals what keeps us apart. Same trees are emptied and refilled. Metal eyes on every wall see what is.

New grows under the shadow of what was. Bright yellows and greens grow from the husks. A new line is sewn onto the tapestry in liquid concrete. What could we be?

ONE LANE CLOSED DUE TO INCIDENT:

A RANDOM SAMPLE OF INCONGRUOUS OBSERVATIONS DURING A FOUR-MILE TAILBACK ON THE M40 BETWEEN JUNCTIONS 6 & 5, 12TH JULY 2022, AT APPROXIMATELY 1.02PM.

JO CLARK

We edge forwards in jagged clutch-controlled tempo, not quite in sync, but together nonetheless, held in place by the unspoken bonds of the tailback, a random three-lane community, thrust together by unexpected inertia. All we have in common is the here and the now, the hot tarmac, the gantry flashing '50 advisory' (though none of us can do more than five, and only then in staccato unison), and the need to be somewhere else, somewhere not here, somewhere unconnected to this tarmac, that gantry, one another.

To our right, a shiny Range Rover, new plates, like it rolled right off the production line into this jam, followed by a metallic-blue soft-top MX5 that from up here in the van looks more toy than car. I stare at the occupants' heads and wonder why Noddy and Big Ears never needed sun cream.

To the left, a flatbed carries an alien constellation of hydraulic equipment, all awkward elbows in industrial orange. Behind it, the pillar box livery of a Royal Mail van hoards greetings and condolences, tax demands and exam results – all belated by the same cause that holds us here. And beyond it, something blood-red glints from deep within the thick peroxide-blonde of summer-long verge-grass and the rusty spires of curly dock. I think it's a poppy, but as we draw level I see it's just a lonely displaced traffic-cone.

On the northbound carriageway, meteor showers of traffic flash past unimpeded, an ever-shifting parade of familiar and new. Supermarket lorries and pantechnicons, a Megabus and the gravity-defying geofolded mountain ranges of car transporters… vans and cars and caravans… vans and cars and lorries. A stream, a flood, but not a community. Nothing to bind them, they float free and alone in their one-way universe.

In front of us, Jack.

Tired tarpaulin in egg-yolk-yellow, ingrained with the grime of many motorway miles. Dated burgundy lettering, proclaiming a landline number (no website):

Watkinsons General Haulage – Great Missenden.

You are following Jack.

One of the best.

I wonder if Jack is aware of us, sees us in his mirrors. I imagine he's been doing this for so long, it's routine. I imagine he's belonged to so many tailback communities over the years that it's all as much a blur to him as the northbound stream. He's not far from home; I imagine a wife waiting, making his favourite tea, ironing his polo shirt and hoping he'll cut the lawn tomorrow on his day off, it's looking a bit long again.

I imagine photo frames of grinning grandkids on the mantel, a favourite mug for his coffee. Annual holidays with one or other of the grown-up children. Counting down the years, not long to retirement now, if only the government would keep diesel down, he could do it in three, but the way it's going, with everything else going up, it's looking more like five. The tutting. The shaking of a head. Making another cuppa to wash down the disappointment. Shaking out the crease in the newspaper to read the cricket scores.

I watch two red kites circling overhead, forked rudder-tails and gracile movement unmistakeable. Tiny mannikins walk the chalk path high to the left, rounding the hill at Aston Rowant.

We edge forward again, and Jack wobbles out of lane, dangerously close to the tiny blue toy car. Only for a fractured second; he recovers quickly, and by the time we're stationary again, he's back on track.

But I'm not.

One of the best.

Are you though? I wonder. Are you still one of the

best, Jack? Or are you losing it. My confidence in Jack is fractured.

As we pass the incident (navy and white cab, silver tanker, white paint pooling into the hard shoulder to form a milky river down the hill ahead of us) our tiny community disperses, a galaxy blown apart as suddenly as it formed. I decide I'll wave to Jack when we inevitably pull out and pass him.

But Jack turns off at the next junction, and I'm left watching the soaring kites, twisting in the high Chiltern skies.

Be safe, Jack, I whisper.

CURIOUSER AND CURIOUSER

BECK COLLETT

"Come on, it's easy enough. Even you should be able to follow!"

"You know I hate games, though."

"It isn't a board game, though, or a card game. We aren't playing hide and seek, or joining in online with the weirdo role-players. Come on, Jessie, just one try? It'll be fun."

Jessie hated games. I know you'll already have grasped that, but it bears repeating. Anything that involved her being put in a position where she could statistically lose was outside of her remit. It wasn't that she wasn't any 'fun', Jessie liked 'fun' as much as the next girl, it was just that potentially losing (especially in front of others) wasn't 'fun' to her. For all the genuine warmth, charisma, and spontaneity you'd experience, spending time with Jessie Kellerman was like being locked in a room with a robot. Though that may be a little hard on robots, what with scientific advances and all.

However, Jessie found Marcus rather intoxicating, and was conscious of how repellent a girl could seem when she wouldn't play games. She eyed the table, feeling faint, concerned that her breakfast would make a grand entrance if she didn't turn and run. But she didn't, and that made Jessie feel very good about herself indeed. "Okay," she breathed, "tell me the rules, and maybe I'll have one go. Just one, though, Marcus, I haven't time to waste on frippery and nonsense, as you well know."

Marcus *didn't* 'well know' anything. That wasn't an exaggeration. It was fortunate, Marcus' mother would say, that he was blessed with an angelic face, because his head and heart may as well have been filled with sawdust for all the knowledge they possessed. Fortunately, his handsome chops were enough to allow him to get by, and were more than enough for him to show off his new game to breathless schoolgirls.

Marcus had come across the game while trawling the web at three in the morning, elated from having won an online battle slaughtering orcs, and with his dad's credit card in hand. Whereas you or I may have woken the next day with a bad head, and an email screaming that we had bought a shoddily sewn dress for the bargain price of £3.99, made of itchy material, with the wrong colour thread on the seams, which would look absolutely *nothing* like the pictures once it arrived, Marcus awoke to find he'd bought a game of chance from a website that didn't exist. You or I, certainly Jessie, would have panicked that said non-existent website had our dad's credit card details, and confessed first thing, but that didn't occur to Marcus. He merely smiled, shrugged, and trotted off to the bathroom to do three other things beginning with S.

But now he had a willing player (at last!) to try out the odd item that had come via a tired courier in a dirty white van three days previous. He grinned at Jessie. "Simple game, Jessie, fifty-fifty chance of winning. All you have to do is close your eyes, put your hand in the jar, and pull out a pill. Fifty-fifty chance of it being a win, a blank sugar-pill, in which case you pop it in your mouth and eat it. Easy."

"But, if it's fifty-fifty, and a sugar-pill is the win, what is the loss?" asked Jessie, who was no fool.

"Well," Marcus stammered, having only scanned the intricately folded instructions sheet, (in his defence, it was written in very mangled English, and began with the legend: 'Dearest Friend, we hope this finds you well!'). "Well, should you lose, Jessie, and pull out a loss, a fu-, sorry, an effed-up pill, then you swallow it, and the world grows a little bigger."

Jessie stared at him in surprise. This wasn't what she had expected, more something along the lines of the foul-tasting jellybeans her nephew always had on him. "Well... that doesn't sound like a loss, Marcus, the world growing bigger. Scary, I suppose, but more places to explore, should the right companion ever come along. Are you sure that's it? Sugar or growth?"

Marcus nodded, pleased he had managed to persuade someone to play. He himself hadn't dared, after his mother had read down to the final instruction, and banned him from playing it. She'd said something about it being *too Alice for words*, but Marcus didn't know an Alice, so hadn't thought it applied. Anyway, "Close your eyes, Jessie," he instructed, "and pop your hand in the jar."

Jessie did as she was told, and pulled a blank sugar-pill.

"Well done," Marcus said. "Round two."

Another blank sugar-pill.

"Good-oh," said Marcus, through slightly gritted teeth. "You aren't cheating, are you, Jessie?"

"Of course not," Jessie giggled. "It's just beginners' luck."

On and on they played, until round eleven, when Marcus got his wish, and Jessie pulled an effed-up pill from the jar. "Oh, no, Jessie, you effed-up! Well, rules are rules, and the world will grow a little bigger, remember?"

Jessie popped the pill in her mouth. It melted at once on her tongue. The funny thing was that it tasted of cherry-tart and custard at first, then left an aftertaste of roast turkey! Jessie giggled again. "Delicious. Can I have another go, or is it game over?"

"No," Marcus replied. "Have as many goes as you wish, Jessie."

And she did. Jessie managed to pull four sugar-pills (though the taste was getting a little hard to swallow) and six effed-up pills. Each time the effed-up pill melted, it tasted different.

"Mmm, buttery toast," Jessie squeaked, her mouth

stuffed full to burst, "and toffee! Lovely. How far through the jar have I got now, Marcus?"

"Only five more to go," he replied. "Shall I pass them to you, Jessie?"

"No, no, I want to do it properly." And Jessie popped the first four in, one after another. All sugar-pills. "I shall be diabetic after this," she laughed.

Marcus didn't laugh, he just watched as she swallowed the last pill. "You effed-up there, Jessie," he said, fumbling off her blindfold.

Jessie stared in horror as she saw that the world had grown much bigger – sort of. When you shrink to five inches tall, everything looks much bigger, you know.

"Sorry, Jessie," Marcus said, "but I have to put you in the jar now. Rules are rules." And he did just that.

THE IDEA OF TUESDAYS
JACOB COOK

SCENE 1. EDWARDIAN STREET:

A backdrop of Edwardian London: one crooked lamppost. Members of THE MILLER FAMILY (to be seen later) can fill the backdrop in lieu of extras.

A girl wanders through the street, dressed as a maid. This is THE CLOSING GIRL – meek, invisible, not ready to speak.

Not yet.

Monday night had been spectacular. This, however, was Tuesday.

Geoff had worked as a job centre coach for seven years now. Possibly eight. Or twenty-four. He'd taken up the role with such innocuous mediocrity that every day had blurred into one continuous, futile stream. Truthfully, not a single client had ever left his service feeling helped or enlightened, and there was nothing in his life to justify a story being told – which is why this isn't about him.

It's about the young woman sitting across from him, faking eye contact through perspex.

"Have you considered..."

She tuned out the rest of the sentence, filling in amusing possibilities in her head. Mime artist. Hill inspector. Dolphin fluffer. They'd danced this merry jig more times than she'd had hot dinners, her immovable object countering his unchangeable force. She'd smile, and nod, and send off one application for something far out of town while faking another four to placate the Work & Pensions gods. Geoff didn't check anyway. He'd not commented on 'Personal Assistant to Judi Dench'.

"Or what about this?" Geoff swivelled his screen, a long job description blurring into blah blah blah. "Remember, you're getting Universal Credit, but you're always better off in work. Always."

She took a brief glance. "That's volunteer work. Unpaid."

Blink blink. "Well, we're running over a little, so I think we'll call it there."

Oh, I bet we will.

Life for Cynthia Norton was a twisted game of dreams weighed down by reality. Except once, so recently, those dreams had come true.

Her town was an artistic graveyard, the archetype used to symbolise a protagonist's world of futility. Its one claim to culture was the dilapidated theatre stitched to the side of a leisure centre, long since resigned to cover artists of cover artists. The stage was set for local director Flynn Swain to make his mark.

The play was called 'The Closing Girl', with Cynthia in the titular role. Servant of the Miller household under a vow of silence for ambiguous reasons never entirely explained, who declared (via typewriter) that said vow would be broken at midnight. A gathering was held to commemorate the occasion, the rich and powerful family entranced by what their silly maid might say. Somehow, that wouldn't be the most striking revelation of the evening, which was as much as Flynn would ever give away before opening night. This was to be seen to be believed.

Centre stage wasn't destined to be hers. She skulked away in the background, set-dressing as this world revolved around her, secrets spilled by people desperate to fill the silence. She wasn't the protagonist. She was a black hole to destroy their universe. As Act One bled into Two, bleeding into blood itself across the creaking floorboards, still she waited until the curtain's fall – it actually descended, the audience thrown, before rising again to reveal her, finally. She had just twenty-seven words. And made every single one of them count.

Three nights and then the wrap party, eighteen cast and crew crammed into Flynn's miniscule flat, drinking, laughing, reminiscing on the past while it stood borderline to the present, Cynthia making doe eyes at the leading lady a tad too old for her…

As the sky grew light, it brought the beginning of a

slow walk home. But not yet. Flynn lived right by the theatre, insight flying through his window like fairy dust. Cynthia now stood amidst the veil's divide. Stepping out, stepping away, was a concession, a promise to move on from the best night of her life.

So she closed her eyes. One. Entering a complete state of absence, the world fell away, leaving only her in an endless void. Two. A playbill in hand, a poster on the wall emblazoned with her name, and still, it was all history. Three. Open. Done. The week went on with aeons behind and nothing ahead.

Geoff's appointment over, Cynthia followed her instincts, wandering back onto the streets for an empty afternoon. The job centre also bordered on the theatre, so she struck up a cigarette, leaning against the wall, probably looking to any passer-by like scum who couldn't be trusted to clean the aisles. Who cared? Not her.

Did he?

There was someone watching her, head tilted to the side like he was trying to place a face. He glanced left, to the poster. Face placed.

"Sorry, sorry… are you Cynthia Norton?"

She couldn't place him in return. "So it's been said. Do I know you?"

"You do not. But I loved you in…" He squinted. "The Closing Girl. Loved you! Your big monologue… ah, chills!"

Smoke went down the wrong way. A fan, an honest-to-goodness fan? She studied him further: messy hair, crooked glasses, a glazed grin shared by the illegally medicated. Someone in this town knew her name. Geoff didn't know her name; her parents didn't know she'd changed it to sound more 'showbiz'. Yet this stranger, with his crumpled clothes and giddy gaze, was certain of it.

The stranger filled the shock. "Oh, of course – where are my manners? Pascal, Pascal Pascoe. Call me Pascal, call me Pascoe, all I need is the first half of the name, eh?" His left sleeve, rolled up four folds precisely, began to slip down. He corrected its position without looking. "Let me guess. You're looking for work."

"How do you know?"

"You're an actor. They spend more time searching than working. And as luck would have it, I'm looking for a leading lady. Can I tempt you?"

Before she could answer, her hands were touching paper.

ROUTINE

By Pascal Pascoe

Shooting Script

She looked again, but Pascal was speed-walking off into the distance at the pace of an overly confident gay man. "You've got my number!" he shouted back.

"I do?"

"If you read to the end!"

Alright then. That's what she'd have to do.

SCENE 6. ATTIC:
EILEEN and MARVIN MILLER look through a PHOTO ALBUM.

MARVIN:
Such a silly little boy. Always the runner.

EILEEN:
I'm surprised he sat still for these.

MARVIN:
I seem to remember rope being involved.

They laugh – but Eileen stops, confused.

MARVIN (CONT'D):
What?

EILEEN:
The picture. That's not him.

'Routine' was a tragic yet beautiful tale. That was what Pascal said to anyone who would listen and Cynthia found it hard to disagree. A young girl, trapped on the slow path of life, meets a boy going too fast. No romance, but such a fascination between the two, a mutual belief that one could stabilise the other. She'd never read anything like it. Better yet, she was right in the centre from the start – sorry, Flynn, she wasn't waiting her turn today.

In fact, she wasn't waiting at all. Pascal had gleefully cast her the moment she'd texted, his number indeed chicken-scratched right below the final line, hers once more: 'It's a brand new day.'

Filming was ready to begin in less than forty-eight hours for four days straight; she'd been awake all night whispering lines into the mirror. Did her new identity of 'Lyra Tarbuck' need to look completely sleep-deprived? Surely it was subtext.

Day one was an outdoor shoot, a charming break from the clammy theatre hall. It didn't take long to find them: Pascal's energy lit up the park from fifty paces, not to mention the obvious indicator of cameraman Shehrz, a bleary-eyed chap whose focus was fixed entirely down the lens. Introductions came and went in a blur, Pascal eager to kick things off.

"Burning daylight, people." Pascal's enthusiasm shifted into barely hidden control. The director was in. "Where's Mark?"

"Taking a wazz," Shehrz chipped in. "He'll be back… now, actually."

Cynthia turned to see another man strolling across the grass: a bit tall, bit broad, maybe a bit pretty if she didn't order off the vegan menu. Her co-star had arrived.

"Hi." He conducted himself with immediate professionalism. "You must be Cynthia. I'm Mark. Ready to make a film?"

"Ready as I'll ever be," she smiled, platonically charmed. "You know, I've never made one before."

"Well, we've all gotta start somewhere."

"Not your first time then?" God, she regretted the wording as soon as it came out of her mouth. "I mean…"

"No and no." Mark matched the smile. "I've made a few, one or two along with Calcoe here."

"Calcoe?"

"Better than Paspas!" Pascal leapt into the conversation like any given side character diving for a bullet. "Old nickname among old friends, ha." He actually said 'ha'. "You can call me that too! But later. Scene three, take one, let's go in ten."

"Oh, er…" What was her line? Her blocking? Suddenly all eyes were on her; she could feel the public boring into her art as they walked on by. Calm down. Films had second takes for a reason. This was only the beginning.

Pascal had dipped behind the camera, Mark running out of shot as he twirled his hands. "Three, two, one…"

Silver screen, here she came.

SCENE 10. DINING ROOM:

WILBUR stands tall at the revelation, MARVIN enraged.

MARVIN:
You took her from me!

WILBUR:
She was never yours.

Day two of filming was in Pascal's house: grubby and unfurnished. "Set dressing!" he called it, Cynthia concluding that taking him at his word was the safest option. After all, her first day had been wondrous, blurring together in the joy of the medium. Set or not, it looked good on camera. Or bad. Whatever the critics said. Oh god, would this get reviewed?

"Right right! Into position, let's get going."

Pascal wasn't having any of her panic, raring to go. Something seemed a little off about him today, not that she had much to go on. His usual buzz seemed to have shifted, not up or down but to the side, resulting in a sheer incomprehensibility, even considering his norm. Whatever. So long as he could still direct.

"Right right, okay." She checked her script. "Isn't Mark in this scene?"

Shehrz looked awkward without looking, a shift of the shoulders speaking sentences. Pascal meanwhile didn't blink. At all.

"Did I not text you?"

She was sure he hadn't, yet felt a need to check.

"Mark's… erm… dropped out. He had some… creative disagreements."

"Really? The script's wonderful."

The twinkle of an ego tickled. "Too kind, too kind. Anyway, the show must go on."

"So who's playing Hamish?"

Cue spotlight. "Me!"

'Taika Watiti' flashed through Cynthia's mind.

"I know, I know." Pascal styled it out like a modest tech conglomerate. "I know exactly what you're thinking. Can I act? Shehrz, can I act?"

"No."

The squeak of his turning heel was painful to nearby dogs. "I'm sorry?"

"You take on every role so well you become them. It would be wrong to call it acting," Shehrz clarified, as deadpan as a murdered wok.

"Exactly!"

Cynthia coughed. "Actually, I was going to ask what we're doing about yesterday's scene."

"We'll cut it." Not beaten for a second. "T'was a force majeure, but we'll make do. Three! Two! One!"

And in. "Hamish, why–"

"Cut!" Pascal raised his hands. "Pascal... not good enough. That facial expression, completely wrong for the mood. Sorry, Cynthia, I do apologise for him. Again?"

SCENE 13. FLASHBACK – GARDEN:
EILEEN sits on a park bench, nervous, next to a BUSINESSMAN, an expensive suit masking a shark's gaping jaw.

BUSINESSMAN:
I wonder what would catch Marvin's attention, hmm?

EILEEN:
He likes a good dresser.

BUSINESSMAN:
An expensive dresser. A sack would do him so long as it was woven from gold. And the Nook family finds itself in hard times. Shall we discuss terms?

Day three – or technically, night one, summoned to the back streets. Yesterday had been put out of Cynthia's mind for the sake of sanity. Alright, Pascal was eccentric. Artists were; even Flynn would dance around the stage like a possessed heron. So long as he didn't go full Kubrick – or worse, full Weinstein – all was fine. A ticket out no matter the transport.

"Cynthia, have you read today's rushes?" Current Pascal level: Michael Bay.

"I glanced over them."

"I can tell. There were a few overnight changes. Go on, take five."

"It's take three."

"Thank you, Shehrz."

Scrolling through her phone, she spotted the rewrites. Oh no. Heterosexuality. Overnight, he'd ripped apart the entire plot and reassembled the scrapes into a conceited self-insert romance, any depth her character possessed shuffled into battering eyelashes. Ruined. But what could she do? Writer ruled all. On she went.

Not only had the script been changed, it had been lengthened, scene after scene flying past in sheer incoherency. This was no longer art, it was the plumber before the naughty stuff. Midway through some rambling along the lines of 'Oh Hamish, your eyes hold the wisdom of a thousand stars', she paused. "Pascal, don't you think this is maybe a bit much?"

She'd never seen someone truly freeze before. Like she'd pressed 'pause' on his whole body. "Much?"

"I mean, it's all great. But the first draft was just a little more subtle, and a few words can go a long way…"

"Much." Kubrick. "You've not written before, have you? No, thought not. You're new to all this. And that's fine. I love working with… new talent. Maybe remember that fact, hmm hmm?"

And she thought of her parents, and she thought of Geoff, and she thought of the applause.

"Yeah. Sure."

"Glad we cleared that up." He smiled. "And again."

SCENE 18. DINING ROOM:

MARVIN crosses the room, shaking THE CLOSING GIRL.

MARVIN:

What have you done?

Silence. Still she refuses to speak.

MARVIN (CONT'D):

Tonight of all nights! You've torn this family apart.

WILBUR:

She hasn't said anything!

MARVIN:
Exactly! Never in all the time she's been here. Dragged her up from nothing, gave her purpose, then what does she do? Judges. All those looks from the corner. Everything crumbles like secrets in a fireplace. And nothing happens to you.

One more day. Pascal had sent through the rushes, and as she'd expected, this was ending in a kiss. Nuance had exited stage right. Fine. Fine. Artistic integrity versus her only escape, Monday night on a different stage. She'd googled 'force majeure' before coming, with several spellings. Praying for one of those now. Her lover boy was even cheerier than usual. She couldn't think why.

"We have one shot at this," he was rambling, his toothy smirk resembling a skull before dental surgery. "Festival deadline is Thursday, and Shehrz can edit that fast but sure as hell can't film it."

"This is for a festival?"

"Oh, didn't I say?"

No. Just say action, by all that's holy.

LYRA: I don't understand. Why does it have to end like this?

HAMISH: Because it was always meant to. Because there's nothing we can do to save each other.

LYRA: Two souls, only destined to cross paths.

HAMISH: And never cross over.

LYRA: So what do we do?

HAMISH: Enjoy the intersection.

Hamish – Pascal – shut his eyes, leaning in…

Marvin's distracted; he turns.

Missing her reach towards the table… the sharpest KNIFE *on display.*

LYRA: I'm sorry, 'Hamish'. But no.

HAMISH: …What?

LYRA: No.

HAMISH: That's, er… that's not what you're meant to say.

LYRA: Well, I'm saying it.

HAM-CAL: Okay, I think we need to try again-

CYNTH-YRA: Why? We've crossed the intersection. You've moved too fast. Maybe I move too slow, or maybe you never learned to walk at anybody else's pace, never listened to what they had to say.

PASCAL: Listen here. I'm in charge, we're doing this my way-

CYNTHIA: Doesn't look like it, does it?

PASCAL: No, stop! This is my story!

CYNTHIA: And you let me tell it. Which is why it ends now. It's a brand new day.

And with that, she rose, and she left. Shehrz had the presence of mind to pan to the door, catching its slam perfectly in frame. Pascal stood, as if to follow, then stopped, the tiniest glance to camera. "We can use that, right?"

Shehrz just shrugged, silence the most damning criticism. The grin began to slip from Pascal's eyes.

Thirty seconds later, Cynthia was out the door, daring to look back at the upstairs window.

Where Pascal was aiming the camera, framing her perfectly.

"So… what have you been up to this week?"

"Oh, not much."

And here she was again. Like a bad dream, except the waking world wasn't too much cheerier with the appointed dimwit. She let Geoff ramble, autofilling responses. Now this was routine. Too late for a rewrite?

Monday, she'd taken an early night, the world leaving

her to slog through the week until it came back round, longer than seven days ought to be. There was a poetic way to put that, however it didn't come to phrase – after all, she'd never written before.

"Right. Same time again?"

Some lines were in every draft. Geoff was a fixed point in history: immortal and unkillable. Their battle of witlessness would go on for a long time yet. To grin and bear it was the only solution, in the knowledge that there was a way out, one day, on the strike of midnight. And the clock was ticking. She'd make her true feelings known somehow.

"Sure. See you next Tuesday."

SCENE 21. DINING ROOM:

The grandfather clock rings out as the room stands empty. THE CLOSING GIRL enters.

For a moment, all is still. She begins to dust, before stopping, addressing the audience directly, slow.

THE CLOSING GIRL: You waited. Why?

(pause)

Silence has its advantages. Talk too much and you'll be heard. Speak only when necessary. Always when necessary. They'll learn. And so will you.

WEARING RAGS AND FEATHERS

JO DERRICK

Suzanne was a one-off. I certainly had never met anyone like her when in 1982 I walked into that back-to-back terrace in Headingley, hoping that the three students living there would offer me a room.

Her boyfriend, Red, answered the door. He was wearing one of those Army and Navy store khaki coloured parka coats with a German flag emblem on the sleeve. The small kitchen reeked of boiled cabbage and cat. They'd recently adopted a kitten, which Suzanne had found shivering in a box next to the bins halfway up the street. They named him George and he hadn't been out of the house since.

"You're the first person to come and look at the room," was the first thing Suzanne said to me. "Cup of tea? Coffee?"

My eyes were drawn to the small kitchen counter

covered with stains, toast crumbs, stray cornflakes and knives smeared with butter.

"No, thanks. I haven't got much time to spare. I've a lecture at two."

She was curled up on the small red two-seater sofa, her long, slim legs tucked under her. She was idly wafting a peacock feather with one hand, the other resting on the pages of an open book. She didn't appear to have any intention of moving.

"Red will show you the room. We gave it a bit of a clean yesterday. I'm afraid it was home to a pigeon with an injured wing for a while, but I think we've got most of the marks off the wallpaper and carpet."

I felt like turning around and walking out the door, but Red stood behind me, his arms folded across his chest like some kind of security guard.

He smiled. He had nice eyes and generous lips. I wondered what they'd be like to kiss.

"Follow me," he said and led me up a narrow staircase with a worn and filthy orange carpet.

On the first landing two doors faced each other.

"That's ours," he said, gesturing to the open one.

I glimpsed a bundle of clothes on the floor, then turned to follow him as he opened the other door, the outside of which was covered with a poster of Che Guevara.

The room was large and, on the plus side, it had a washbasin. I was expecting the same level of shabby Seventies' decor as the kitchen and stairs, but someone had taken a bit more trouble with this room. It had recently been painted white and instead of a threadbare carpet, there were bare boards covered in rag rugs.

"Gaynor, the last girl, was the creative sort," said Red, once more with his arms folded across his chest. "She painted the room a couple of months before she left. She even left behind the rugs she'd made. Spent hours sitting on her bed sewing and stuff. I think she was a bit bonkers, to be honest, but Suzanne liked her. She used to feed Suzanne tea and mandarin oranges. I think they were lovers for a while."

He said it so casually that I almost missed it. I was shocked. Back in Croydon I'd never heard of two girls being lovers. I was a Second Year student, studying Classics and I'd spent my first year in a dreary all-girls Halls of Residence, which was how I imagined a boarding school to be. I didn't really click with anyone and spent most of my time in my room, studying and playing Joni Mitchell songs.

"Do you like it?"

"Sorry?"

"The room. Do you like it? Fancy living here?"

I walked around a bit, trying to imagine myself being here day-in, day-out. I went up to the window and looked out onto the street. The house opposite seemed within touching distance and, further up, lines of washing were strung high above the road, white sheets billowing in the breeze. A couple of Asian ladies in bright pink saris were chatting on the pavement.

"I'd like to meet the other people who live here. Are they in?"

"Nope. They have lectures. Couple of swots."

"What are their names?"

"Mick and Chris. Both doing Engineering. Boring as."

Just then Suzanne appeared in the doorway. "Like it?"

"It's a nice room. How much?"

It was the cheapest I'd looked at so far. "I'll take it."

I was thinking more about the money I'd save than whether I'd actually get on with these people.

Suzanne clapped her hands in delight. "And you haven't even seen the bathroom yet!"

My heart sank. I'd forgotten all about the bathroom. It was a dark little room on the same landing. The window looked as if it had never been cleaned and the walls were covered in peeling orange paint. There was a bath, but no shower, and a toilet with a wonky seat. The washbasin was covered in shaving stubble and dried soap. The enamel in the bath was chipped and badly stained. I wondered whether I could back out.

"We get showers at the Uni gym," said Suzanne. "If I want a bath, I usually go to a mate's house. It's no big deal. Sometimes I go a fortnight without either. It does get a bit cold for strip washes in the winter, though."

Of course there wasn't any central heating. Few houses back then had it, especially in back-to-backs in Leeds. I thought about home down in Croydon and how Mum and Dad always kept the place cosy and snug. That familiar pang of homesickness nestled somewhere beneath my ribs and I had the urge to burst into tears. I pictured my parents and brother sitting at the dining table eating a roast dinner and longed for a 'beam me up, Scotty'-type device to ping me over there right that minute.

I noticed Red trying not to laugh as he stood back near the top of the stairs. I couldn't work him out. Was he arrogant? A bit of a joker? A narcissist? What? That was the trouble when you were searching for a room in a shared house, there wasn't the time to get to know the people you'd be living with. Another problem with not having an established group of friends to share with, like most of the others on my course.

They gave me a rent book and we arranged a time for me to move my stuff in. It would soon be the start of the summer break, but I still had to pay a reduced rent before I moved in properly in the autumn. It didn't seem fair, but that was the way it worked. At least I had a job over the summer working in a bookshop close to my parent's place. I was lucky. Most other students I knew had to work in tacky pubs or one of the new fast food restaurants that had started opening up.

The day I moved in properly, the leaves were just turning to a burnished gold with the edges of green reminding me of the summer just past. I'd met Jim in the coffee shop next to where I worked and we'd had an all-too-brief relationship. He finished it when he had to go back to Bristol for his Final Year. I wasn't in love with him or anything like that, but I still felt sad and regretted how the shape of our love had twisted.

Back at Thorold Grove for the autumn term, Suzanne greeted me with ostrich feathers in her long blonde hair and wearing a collection of what looked like the rags her former housemate, Gaynor, had used to make the rugs.

"Salvation Army shop. Brilliant for bargains. Come with me next time. We can find you something exciting to wear instead of those beige A-line skirts and polo necks. And please don't get into the latest fashion of wearing those ghastly baggy mohair jumpers in primary colours. Hideous!"

There was no sign of Red that day and later, after sharing a bottle of Black Tower wine with Suzanne, I discovered she'd chucked him. I felt a bit sad. I quite liked him. In fact, while I was sitting in my two o'clock lecture an hour after that first time at 52 Thorold Grove, I'd decided I fancied him.

"He was a bit too controlling, you know what I mean?"

I didn't. I thought all men were like that. "It's the men who wear the trousers," my mum had always said or "Your father knows best." I'd never questioned it until Suzanne began to teach me about feminist politics and so much more.

Suzanne introduced me to Leonard Cohen's music. We'd sit cross-legged on her floor, drinking Dry Martinis and sometimes smoking, listening to songs about birds on wires, jazz police and famous blue raincoats. We cried together and held each other when we got maudlin after too much gin. And then somehow I was sleeping in her room more often than my own.

"He could have written that song for me," she mused one cold winter's day as we lay in bed eating toast.

We'd been listening to 'Suzanne', probably his most famous recording. I can't hear it now without crying.

"We should buy a place near the Thames when we get those top jobs in publishing."

"Virago?"

"Absolutely."

We had high ambitions, but didn't ever study hard enough to achieve them on leaving Uni. We both scraped 2:2s, but we were long past caring. Along with George The Cat, we stayed on in Thorold Grove throughout our Final Year and beyond. Other students came and went. Some we got on with, some we slept with and others we couldn't stand, but somehow we became a permanent fixture with PA office jobs in the city centre while still pretending to be students.

It was only when Paul came along that things changed. We interviewed him in August '88. We were beginning to despair of ever finding someone to occupy the second top room. Clive, a Physics graduate, was in the first top room. He wanted to stay on another year while he did his Masters, so I guess it was off-putting to fresh-faced Second Years that we were a house of more mature students. Or not even students in the case of me and Suzanne.

Paul was blond and slight. A bit of a weed, I remember thinking when he first appeared at our door. Despite that, he had a confidence that soared above the red roof tiles of Thorold Grove. He was a third year Medic and he was as beautiful as a sleeping child. There was a serenity about him that drew us all in. He became a worm on a hook as far as Suzanne and I were concerned.

She started writing poetry and pinning the poems up on walls and doors all over the house. It was obvious they were written for Paul, but he seemed oblivious. It was as if nothing could touch him emotionally, yet he didn't come across as cold or aloof. It was as if he was above such common human conditions as love and empathy, yet he adored George The Cat. He was the only one who could coax him outside and feed him tit-bits while cuddling him on the sofa. George had always run a mile from any previous male tenants. We guessed it was because some horrible man had done something to traumatise him as a kitten.

I'd gone home to Croydon for the weekend and when I returned on the Sunday evening, I heard Leonard Cohen playing upstairs. I plonked down my overnight bag on the floor of the postage stamp-sized hallway and took the stairs two at a time. It had been a difficult weekend, as my mother wasn't well and I was eager to feel the comfort of Suzanne's arms around me.

Except she had her arms around someone else.

Paul.

I briefly took in the thin green candles flickering in the tacky candelabra she'd found in the Salvation Army shop, but very little else. Fury snatched at my tears as I ran back down the stairs. I picked up my bag and keys, then slammed the door behind me.

I never went back.

I got that job in a top publishing house specialising in women's books. In fact, I'm now commissioning editor within a stone's throw of a generous retirement package.

Yesterday I received a manuscript addressed to me personally. I'm usually several arms-lengths away from the slush pile and hand such weighty envelopes to my PA, but there was something about this one. It wasn't weighty for a start. The handwriting looked familiar. There was something about the slope of the 't's' and the loops of the 'g's' and 'y's' that resonated.

Suzanne.

I hadn't thought about her for years, then suddenly I was transported back to birds on the wire, her perfect body, the rags and feathers and love in a back-to-back terrace in the North of England.

I tore open the envelope and tissue thin paper spilled out like confetti. Each piece was covered in her elegant handwriting and I wondered whether she still owned the beautiful Mont Blanc pen. I'd never seen Suzanne use a biro. Quink ink and a fountain pen. Always.

The poems spoke of regrets and loss and what might have been. I suspected from the line: *He drifted in on a late summer breeze, but autumn gales blew him straight back out* that her fling with Paul hadn't lasted long. All these years later I'm not sure whether it was jealousy that drove me away or something else entirely. Life had become a little too comfortable and secure.

I still have a couple of the feathers and a few of the 'rags' we used to dress in. They're tucked away at the top of the wardrobe and from time to time I take them out to parade around the bedroom like that proud twenty-something I used to be.

Suzanne was never a great poet, but I don't discard the work she's sent me. I'll buy a pretty box for them on the way home and I will treasure the poems always. It doesn't even occur to me to find her address on the envelope they came in nor to search within its depths for a note. I know I will never see her again. That part of my life is over. She taught me well and I would never have been the person I am today if it hadn't been for Suzanne. However, I caught a kind of darkness from her and now I realise *that* was the real reason I slammed the door of 52 Thorold Grove behind me that Sunday night.

To paraphrase Leonard Cohen: there are cracks in everything but that's how light can get in.

ME AND MR MOONE

JULIE EASLEY

I took off with Jed Moone because of my dad's love letters. I found them in an empty corner of mam's wardrobe when I was playing hide and seek with my kid sister Anna, and we read all of them, hidden away in a little den we made out of our bunk beds. They were delicately bound with a thin white silk ribbon and wrapped in a faded cloth bag and I could sense the urgency in the lines, even as an eleven-year-old kid I could sense that. You could feel it. My dad was a superhero, I knew that 'cos my mam told us every day, and the many men she stepped out with knew too 'cos she told them every day, and the fact that I couldn't recall him at all just made him even more a superhero.

I met Jed Moone on a beach in Spain. It was the summer of '92, the year I was taken on permanently at the hospital and I was celebrating in style with my mate Jenny. She already knew Jed, she'd met him on holiday the year before. "He works here every year," she said, "ya know, Mandy, he left home at fifteen and I think he's been here every summer since." We watched him then, me and Jen, while we lay sunning ourselves, drinking wine straight out of the bottle. He was handing out tickets to people like me and every time he passed a pretty girl I noticed he flexed his muscles like a preening peacock.

Jed Moone is intriguing. He tells me his dad – who he never met – was French or something, and he has a free and easy way about him. He's wild, very wild with crazy long hair that falls in his eyes. His nose is splayed across his face and he chews the skin on the inside of his mouth so his lips are in a permanent pout. I can't take my eyes off him. I can feel his dangerous energy, it's intoxicating and contagious, the kind of energy where you need to come up for air every now and again.

When my holiday was over and me and Jen were leaving, I gave Jed Moone my address. I didn't give him it for any particular reason, other than everyone else was doing it, and if I'm honest I thought that was the last I would ever see of him.

Then in the winter Jed turned up one day. I was just getting on with my life, looking into buying a house, when he turned up and asked if he could stay for a bit. I figured it'd be fun so I said, "Yeah, why not." At first everyone was excited about Jed Moone. He was different and me and my mates took him out a lot and looked after him. One day Jenny was acting weird.

"What's up, Jen?" I asked.

"He's no good, Mand. Be careful."

I thanked her for the warning but what Jen didn't realise was that Jed Moone made my life better. It didn't take her long to move to the sidelines, her tutting just loud enough for me to hear.

We were friends at first, me and Jed, just hanging out and drinking. When I got in from a busy shift at the hospital, he'd have made me some food, we'd sit cross-legged in front of the fire, drinking sherry, talking about everything and nothing.

Then one afternoon we were doing our usual thing of dreaming and talking when we looked at one another across the room. Now, we'd looked at each other a lot over those months, but this was the moment my life changed, not just because we both knew we were about to make love for the first time, for the look wasn't lust or love or anything sexual. No. In that moment, Jed saw me, and no one had ever seen me before and I knew in that moment that nothing would ever be the same again.

As summer got closer, I worried Jed would leave again so I came up with the idea and said to him, "Jed, we should go travelling together," and he looked up and said, "Yeah, alright." At work, I read an article about a place in Australia called Cooktown and I brought the magazine home when my shift ended and read it aloud to Jed. We were laid on the bed at the time, and while I cut out the pictures, he put Pink Floyd on the stereo and we got up and danced around like dreamers do. Then I pinned the pictures to the front door.

"We'll get there," I said, "and every time we leave, we'll see them."

We stared for a while at the perfect blue sky and the beautiful smiley people and I showed Jed on the map exactly where Cooktown was. I pinned that to the door too and circled it with a thick red marker.

So I go and see my mam, who's fretting now because I don't want a mortgage and when I tell her that I'm going travelling to Australia with Jed Moone, she sobs. "I don't understand it at all, Amanda," and she pleads and begs me not to go, sobbing some more.

"I'm not asking you to understand it, Mam."

"What about your job? It took you years to get where you are, and your sister's wedding, Amanda, please…"

"Mam, for god's sake, they have nurses everywhere. I could probably get work in India…"

"INDIA… INDIA! What happened to Australia… INDIA… Oh Jesus, you're gonna die or get kidnapped… I'm never gonna see you again!"

"Stop it, you're treating me like a kid. I'm twenty-five, mam, and I'm sick of this shithole. There's more to life than Middlesbrough, ya know. This might be the only chance I have for some adventure and no matter how bad you try and make me feel, I'm going… to India. A stopover, if you must know, on the way to Australia."

"Anna's wedding?"

"She won't miss me, none of ya will, I'd only get wrecked and show you all up anyway."

"Money? How are…?"

"I've sold me car and have me last month's wages… that's all we need, Mam. I'm gonna get a job in Australia."

"But do you have to go with HIM?"

She went all quiet then and I could see she was trying to hold it together but she wouldn't stop crying so I told her it was like her and dad. That like my dad was her superhero, Jed Moone was mine and she of all people should get that. She didn't get it but she did stop crying and she held me like she'd never ever held me, well, not since my dad died.

The day I resigned from my job at the hospital, I took Jed with me and all my nursing pals said, "You'd better look after her," and he said, "She don't need looking after," and that was that.

I'd got the job because the ward sister gave me a chance when no one else would. She knew I drank too much, one time I even slept through a whole shift, but she overlooked all my faults because underneath them all I was a good nurse. I had a particular penchant for pus. I loved it. And when a patient had a wound full of pus, I got all excited and would clamour to have them. Then came my favourite bit: the unwrapping, where you'd find out what was inside and, for me, well, the gorier and more disgusting the better 'cos then I would dig around and make them all lovely, dressing them appropriately. It was like a beautiful magic trick and it never failed to amaze me, how with just a little intervention, the body healed itself. The satisfaction from that made me feel all warm inside.

But the main reason the sister took me on was 'cos I excelled at dying. A lot of people have died in my life, a lot of people who I've loved, and so that meant when a patient was dying, I acted in a certain way that brought a lot of comfort. I understood. Once, I lay on the bed with a lady who was all alone and held her gently while she died, till her breathing stilled her body, till at last she looked peaceful. Then when her family came and I told them, they enveloped me in their gratitude and we cried together. The sister appreciated that, though some didn't but I couldn't help it. If I was upset or my patients were upset, I showed it.

And when I walked away that day, from the ward where I'd worked for years, I knew that although I loved being a nurse, that right then I loved Jed Moone more. Right then nothing else mattered. Only Jed Moone.

The night we leave, when I go say goodbye to my mam, she has summoned the family jury. All the siblings are lined up on the settee – all frowns and folded arms and I retreat to the bathroom. I splash cool water on my face, moving slightly the bottle of bath oil that is sitting on the windowsill. Years later when I return, I move it back.

THE MOUSE
CHRIS FOXON

Deniz didn't rescue the mouse because he had any particular liking for animals. He just felt a grim need to thwart next door's cat, that yowling, shitting thing. Yet once he'd driven her off with a couple of well thrown stones, he found himself standing over a quivering white mouse, its back legs splayed weirdly. He knew that they were broken, because they looked just like the spokes of his bike wheel after he crashed into Mrs Khan's wall.

The mouse flailed its front paws, scrabbling for purchase on the insipid tarmac, trying to drag itself away. Deniz watched. If it could make it to the scrubland that encircled the tower block, it might have a chance of eluding the cat.

"Go on, fuck off," he said encouragingly.

But it was hopeless. Try as it might, the mouse couldn't heave its broken body forward.

Deniz understood what had to be done. Not wanting

to spoil his boots, which had cost his birthday and Eid money combined, he looked around for something heavy. Instead, he spotted the cat lurking under number 19's ancient Volvo. He didn't dare throw another stone to send it packing; battered as the car was, he'd pay badly for any scratch. There was always someone watching from the block's myriad of windows, someone ready to snitch the instant his dad got back from the hospital. Smug, the cat's lip rolled over its waiting teeth.

In the gleam of those unfurling ivories, Deniz saw the flap of a white coat, recalled adults bustling self-importantly along corridors reeking of bleach. Instinctively he scooped the mouse up, recoiling from the clamminess of its shattered legs. He didn't know if it was blood or if the thing had shat itself. Nonetheless he tightened his grip when the mouse struggled. He was in charge now.

Plodding up the concrete stairs to his flat, Deniz tried to time each step with the mouse's thudding heartbeat. He toyed with the idea of tossing it down the garbage chute, then dismissed it: the cat often prowled the bins for scraps.

He listened carefully before fitting the key in the lock. Silence. His dad must still be out; visiting hours weren't yet over. Just in case, he crossed the hallway in two big strides and slid into his room, deftly flicking the door shut with his heel.

The mouse was frantic, writhing, Deniz's grasp on it slippery. He tipped out the last chocolates from the box he'd sneaked from his mum's bedside table after they took her away, and deposited the mouse. Immediately it curled up, like one of those stupid furry dice dickheads hung in their cars.

It didn't seem likely to move, so he closed the lid and went to wash his hand, now smeared and sticky. Turning the tap, it occurred to him that the mouse would need water, so he filled a small ramekin and added it to the box. The mouse wasn't to die unless he decided it should. Until he decided it should.

•

Observing the mouse over the next few days, Deniz couldn't decide if it was in pain or not, if it wanted to live or not. He didn't know how you were meant to tell. Mostly it just hunched in a corner. At these times he thought it was shrivelling into death. But then it would surprise him, hauling itself to the water bowl, trembling with pain yet driven by something, not just thirst, something greater and even more primitive. Each day Deniz deliberately moved the bowl to the furthest end of the box, and each day the mouse would answer his challenge.

Plus, it only ever shat in the one spot, never where it drank or slept. That must mean something.

So he called it Minnie – he was sure it was a Minnie, not a Mickey; he didn't know why but he was sure – and refreshed the water daily. He even crumbled some cheddar into the box, though it didn't eat any, not that he saw. Mice were meant to love cheese, famous for it, so perhaps Minnie didn't want to live after all.

What came into his mind was that chemistry lesson, the last lesson before he was abruptly pulled out of school, when they'd learned about metals. This mouse was an alloy. People, neighbours mainly, insisted on telling Deniz how brave he was being, but he didn't know what they meant. Whatever he was, it wasn't one thing, one word. Bravery was not a pure metal. The mouse was like that. It was an alloy of misery, fear, loneliness, obstinacy, agony. Everything that apparently added up to bravery.

He moved the water bowl another inch.

•

"Maybe you'll come with me, this time?"

His dad didn't look at him as he spoke, bending his gaze to the scuffed linoleum. Deniz couldn't remember what colour his eyes were. He racked his brains, then realised they could only be brown, like his, because his mum's eyes were green and he hadn't inherited that from her.

His dad waited, until it became obvious there wasn't going to be an answer, then swallowed, phlegmy. "What it is, Deniz, is that you should come." A hesitation, then, "You'll regret it, if you don't. Later. Afterwards."

The words hung limply in the air. Deniz sat still. His tongue thickened. All he could offer was a shrug. He didn't know what else he was meant to do. Nor it seemed did his father, because for ages he just stood there, not saying a word, head bowed. The pose made Deniz want to scream, to fling himself at his father and tear and scratch at him until he finally looked up, but he thought about Minnie recovering in the next room and didn't. Finally, without another word, his dad turned and trailed out the front door. Soon there came the merciful wheeze of the car starting.

Deniz yanked the curtains closed. From all the other windows overlooking the car park people would be watching his dad drive off, alone, again. Let them. He knew that Mrs Khan would give it ten, then knock with a dish 'for the oven'. It was never for Deniz, always for the oven. He'd ignore her this time. He wasn't public property, as some seemed to think. Anyway, there was plenty of cheese left in the fridge, because Minnie still wasn't touching it.

Google hadn't been any help figuring out what treatment she needed. It just presented a map of animal hospitals, glowing blood-red dots which Deniz was determined never to go near. Eventually he decided to slide a pad of toilet paper under her ruined legs, then improvised cotton bud splints. Minnie flinched and twisted as he tied them in place with string, but ignoring her distress he fixed them firmly. Now the bones could heal.

•

His dad started not to come home at nights; apparently the regular visiting hours no longer applied in their case. Deniz would put himself to bed, checking first that Minnie was comfortable in her box. He always left the hall light on. He told himself this was so that his dad could see if he came home late; really, he didn't dare to tiptoe through the darkness from the switch to his bed. Every time he woke up, the hall light would be off and his dad would be clattering around the kitchen, making breakfast. Before he'd never bothered to do more than tip milk over cornflakes; now he'd whip up peppered eggs or lay out scented pastries on the fancy plates with the green rims. Deniz never did more than pick at the food, which was too rich for him; he would roll the pastry crust into pellets to give to Minnie later, not that his dad noticed.

They didn't mention this change in routine, just orbited each other with studied care every morning. Then his dad would leave clutching opaque Tupperware tubs, one containing lunch and the other dinner, and Deniz would retreat again to his room. He'd change the pad under Minnie's rusty white fur, check the cotton bud splints were still tight, then place the bread pellets beside her. He now permitted the water bowl to rest within easy reach, because clearly she couldn't drag herself around in splints.

Then the day stretched ahead for both of them, Minnie in her box, Deniz in his room. He wished he could go to school, that Mr Carmichael hadn't so briskly decided that "with only a few weeks until the summer holidays you might as well take an extended break, have a proper rest and come back fighting fit next term". Might as well. Break. Fighting fit. Deniz hated the breeziness with which certain people talked to him now, as if they could blow the truth away. He tried not to be like that with Minnie.

He googled chemistry lessons and read them out loud. Sometimes he faltered over the convoluted formulae, his mouth clogging with the ugly swill of letters and numbers. Whenever this happened, he'd glance sharply at the mouse, but Minnie seemed just as soothed by his voice whether he was right or wrong. So he'd resume, and together the pair of them would ease through to nightfall.

•

His phone buzzed. Deniz, huddled against a pillow, watched it. Every time a new ring pulsed through its thin frame, the phone would tremble, its sickly blue tint sliding off the faded roses on the wallpaper. He could see the time. 03.18. Beneath it the caller ID: Dad.

He let it go to voicemail. His dad called back immediately. This time Deniz picked up. His hand was still, he noticed, still and steady, not like in films. He let his dad finish speaking, then hung up and got dressed, tugging on his last clean hoodie. He did all this in the dim glow of the hall's solitary bulb; it didn't seem right to turn on his light.

Minnie was awake. He didn't know if the phone had disturbed her or if she just blinked her way through every night. He bent over the box and stripped the splints from her legs, ignoring the mouse's shudder. Had she healed? It didn't matter now.

He picked the box up and thumped down the stairs, not caring whether he disturbed Mrs Khan. The taxi was waiting, engine thrumming impatiently. Before getting into the front seat ("Watch the meter," his dad had remembered to say, right at the end of the call), he lifted Minnie out, tossed the box towards the trash, and put the mouse down exactly where he'd found it. That seemed about as fair as anything.

As the taxi swung out of the car park, its headlights caught the cat, eyes glinting wetly, stalking forward. That was Deniz's last sight before the darkness swallowed everything.

THE COMPETITION
DEAN GESSIE

Tanvi sipped cardamom tea and said, "Can you believe it? Everyone knows you pound the chillies and the garlic and the ginger using a mortar and pestle. That's a child with no education!"

"Shocking!" said Indrani. "You can't win Regionals by pooh-poohing tradition. He put everything in a *blender*!"

"Preparation counts," said Kanita. "Foolish decisions can lose points."

Said Bhagyashree, "I think the boy's name was Salman."

"Well," said Tanvi, "he was clearly swimming upstream, wasn't he?"

Ishaan laughed and agreed, "In over his head!"

It was three months later and the parents of the winning chefs had gathered in the home of Pooja for the finals of Best Cook Junior, Mumbai Edition.

"After all," said Kanita, "the theme of the evening was Mumbai street food. I don't think the vendors have appliances like that. You can't buy a Nutribullet with a handful of rupees."

Said Ishaan, "Salman must think he's sous-chef at the Marriott Mumbai."

Everyone laughed.

Indrani blew her nose and reanimated the conversation, "And did you see how Yellow Dress slit her *ladi pav* in two pieces?"

Ladi pav was a bun for serving the potato vada pav. Yellow Dress was another child contestant who had failed miserably at Regionals.

Said Kanita, "You can't fully cut the ladi pav. It should look like a clam. Did she think she was working at McDonald's?"

Ishaan recited a version of the Big Mac song. "Two all-beef patties, special sauce, lettuce, cheese, pickles and onions on a spongy, eggless bun!"

No one said what they thought, but Ishaan's familiarity with the McDonald's jingle might explain why he had the profile of an egg.

Tanvi returned to the topic of Yellow Dress. "That's a child with no education."

Said Bhagyashree, "Sometimes, you can get too much education. Traditional vada pav is served on a local newspaper. One of the children packed vada pav in her father's copy of the Guardian Weekly."

"Outrageous!" said Ishaan. "No self-respecting street vendor would pack vada pav in the Guardian Weekly. You'd have to give it away."

Every parent laughed, save for Bhagyashree, who was already thinking ahead. "And did you see how the losing kids dressed their bun?"

Ishaan said, "You can't serve vada pav with split buns. Honestly, who has come face to face with split buns?"

One of the parents blushed, but the others launched reproving glances. The conversation had moved on.

"And no one serves a Mumbai vada pav," said Kanita, "with just dry garlic chutney."

"That's traditional," said Pooja, "but that's not Mumbai."

Added Bhagyashree, "You need *meetha* and *teekha* chutney, too!"

Said Indrani, "My Aashna made her own meetha."

"So did Salman," said Bhagyashree, "but he used a pressure cooker."

Said Ishaan, "Salman must think he's sous-chef at the Marriott Mumbai."

All the parents censured Ishaan with disapproving looks. He had the annoying habit of repeating the same jokes, as if each aged like wine.

Eventually, Kanita returned to the main theme. "My Aakesh," she said, "made his meetha chutney with both fennel seeds and cumin seeds."

Ishaan sought to win back favour of any sort. "And he dry-roasted them to perfection. That child's a genius!"

Bhagyashree referred everyone to her daughter's use of the *kadhai*. "Did you see how Saanvi packed her pan with steaming hot sand and potatoes? Now, that's authentic cooking! You couldn't get closer to the streets of Mumbai if you were a dog or a cat or a rat."

To spare the feelings of Bhagyashree, Tanvi steered clear of zoological comparisons. "And did you see," she said, "how my Gita used *three clean knives* to prepare her teekha? Ingredients should not cross-contaminate! Coriander, ginger and chillies should only consummate at the appointed time."

All the parents shared reproving glances with Tanvi who somehow managed to say something wildly esoteric and clearly inappropriate at the same time.

Afterward, Ishaan reinvigorated the appointed theme. "My Pria," he said, "reversed the order of the condiments. She started with *sukhi lehsun ki*, added the teekha chutney and then finished with the meetha chutney. I don't know how she does it! Do the gods inspire her? Does she have a third eye? I expect she'll have her own cooking show before she reaches puberty."

For some time thereafter, five of the six parents played a kind of celebratory ping pong, recounting the reasons for which their children had won Regionals and why the other children had embarrassed their families to the seventh generation. It was only then that someone realized that Pooja had left the room.

"Of course, she's gone," whispered Bhagyashree. "What can she add to the conversation? Her son wasn't there!"

Kanita said, "It was a bargain with the devil."

Effectively, the finals of Best Cook Junior, Mumbai

Edition had been cancelled because of the death of the sponsors in a fiery car crash. This event caused feelings of sorrow, wretchedness and misery, until Pooja offered to host and finance the finals on the condition that her child be granted direct entry. Of course, she and the others agreed to observe the *Teravih*, a traditional mourning period that included thirteen days following the funeral of the deceased. Afterward, the parents proceeded quickly. The children should not suffer for an act of God on the Mumbai-Pune Expressway.

"Whatever the outcome here today," said Bhagyashree, "it was clearly blackmail to include the boy."

"Appalling," said Kanita.

"And why didn't she move the venue," said Bhagyashree, "to more neutral ground?"

"Scandalous" said Ishaan.

"Everyone knows about home pitch advantage," said Bhagyashree. "Arjun will not suffer the same nerves. And surely he's been playing with the equipment until blue in the face."

"Obscene!" said Kanita.

"And what's with this terracotta?" Bhagyashree tapped a clay teacup with her fingernail. "Isn't it supposed to ring lightly if struck?"

"A cheap imitation," said Kanita.

Said Tanvi, "It's all very political is what it is."

Bhagyashree concurred, "Well, our prime minister should give her the Bharat Ratna."

"Of course!" said Indrani. "You can't win the highest

civilian honour for public service without taking kickbacks."

Ishaan added, "And where are the snacks? Is Pooja so rich that she knows nothing of human suffering? Elephants can go days without eating. Do I look like an elephant?"

The parents did not wish to upset Ishaan by naming the elephant in the room. Instead, they continued to gripe at the expense of their hostess. At one point, Kanita got to her feet and examined the Peshawar Oushak rug that covered the marble floor of the den. She inspected the botanical print and earth tones and began to pull back a tasselled end. She thought she noticed something odd.

Just then, Pooja appeared from nowhere as if her footsteps only existed in a sound stage. "Have you discovered my fault?" she said.

Kanita dropped the rug and took her seat. Each of the parents was traumatized. Had Pooja overheard their criticism? Were they guilty of muddying philanthropy with fault-finding? Pooja's son, Arjun, was not the sharpest tool in the pantry. Surely, there was no harm in letting him play with his food? Anyway, each guest fell over the other with apology. After all, Pooja and her husband, Sunjoy, had been listed in India Today Magazine as one of Mumbai's Top 25 Power Couples. They were not to be insulted.

But what Pooja heard or didn't hear was immaterial. She peeled back the Peshawar Oushak rug and announced with great pride, "I was talking about *this* fault!"

The other parents stared at a huge crack in the floor that was absolutely astonishing.

Said Pooja, "When we moved to Malabar Hill, the agent drew our attention to this fault line. It's one of ten in Mumbai and it goes twenty kilometres deep. If there's ever an earthquake, we'll be the first ones swallowed into the earth and swept out to sea!" And then Pooja abruptly resettled the carpet and announced that she would retrieve snacks from the kitchen.

Ishaan, who had only lately questioned the hospitality of his hostess, quickly called out, "So unnecessary and so generous!"

Once Pooja was out of earshot, Kanita posed a question that was on everyone's mind. "If she's hiding a crack like that in plain sight, what else is she hiding? If Arjun wins this competition, I'll sue. I'll go all the way to the Supreme Court."

Kanita had started to hyperventilate. Bhagyashree gave her a pillow slip to place over her head and instructed her to take long, deep breaths. "Just pretend," she said, "it's the neck-hole of Gordon Ramsay's T-shirt."

Tanvi said, "We have nothing to worry about. Our judge is a famous, well-respected judge with no ties to any of us."

Ishaan said, "It's impossible to cheat. All of the tasting will be anonymous."

Tanvi added, "And no one knows the secret ingredient."

"But," said Indrani, "why can't you hear Pooja when she comes and goes?"

Said Bhagyashree, "She's as stealthy as a ninja. Only people who are hiding something make no noise."

All the parents provided examples of people who hide things quietly.

Nonetheless, the group shared grudging nods that seemed to confer legitimacy to the proceedings. Only then, Kanita removed her head from the imagined neck-hole of Gordon Ramsay's T-shirt and said, "Now, I have an appetite for dessert!"

Effectively, Pooja had returned as quietly as before and placed a tray on the coffee table. She described the snacks as "simple treats" that she had "whipped up" that morning. In effect, Pooja's guests saw *sandesh*, a milk-based confection meaning 'good news'; *jalebi*, a sweet snack made with fermented batter; and *gulab jamun*, fried doughnut balls. The parents immediately swooped down like vultures over a Parsi burial ground.

Bhagyashree said, "I have not eaten jalebi like this since I was a child."

And Ishaan said the lentil powder was perfectly mixed.

Indrani heaped praise on the sandesh and made a religious joke that assumed some scholarship. "The *good news* of the sandesh is the gospel *truth*!"

Speaking of the *gulab jams*, Kanita said, "I hope to die with these syrupy balls in my mouth."

And Tanvi said, with a mixture of admiration and resignation, "Well, these are street drugs, aren't they?"

But Pooja appeared to have difficulty processing the effusive praise. While one of her guests talked about *curdling the milk with lemon*, Pooja emitted a blood-curdling scream.

Arjun had arrived from the room designated for *makeup and hair*. His mother was mortified.

"My god! My son! What have they done to you?"

It was a vintage poodle cut with hair upswept into a poof and curls combed to the side. Pooja ran to her son, grabbed his hand and whisked him away, presumably to somehow undo the hairdo on his head. The parents used the afterward to draw conclusions and air grievances.

"Well," said Bhagyashree, "that boy's finished."

Said Tanvi, "You can't win Best Cook Junior, Mumbai Edition looking like a poodle."

"Unless, of course," said Kanita, "there is a category for Best in Show!"

All the parents laughed and expressed sympathy for Pooja, but not for her cooking.

Of the sandesh, Tanvi said, "My daughter would have garnished with chopped pistachios."

Indrani said, "My daughter would have used saffron."

Ishaan said, "I don't like lumps of lentil powder in my jalebi. Pria would have whisked until she had broken her wrists!"

Bhagyashree said, "Saanvi would have used cardamom rose syrup."

Kanita said, "My boy would have used orange-flower water!"

And Tanvi added, "I'm telling you right now, that gulab

jamun has milk powder. Gita would have used *khoya*! You need milk solids for a soft doughnut."

Just then, Kanita reached beneath the coffee table and surfaced the wedding album of Pooja's eldest daughter. At one particular page, she appeared to be praying fervently, having repeated the words *my god* a dozen times. The others looked, too, and those who weren't struck dumb also parroted the words, *my god.* In effect, one of the photos depicted a wedding guest with his arm around Pooja's daughter. At present, this particular guest was known to everyone as the contest judge.

Outrage was like a five-alarm fire, but Indrani tried to douse the flames. She suggested that Pooja might be ignorant of the relationship.

Tanvi was having none of it. Her face appeared to pucker with bitter gourd. "Trust me," she said, "a mother knows the name and address of any man that has ever laid hands on her daughter."

"*And*," said Bhagyashree, "who do you think made the guest list?"

"Well," said Kanita, "the *fix* is clearly in."

"We can all safely assume," said Ishaan, "that Arjun knows the secret ingredient."

"Or if he doesn't," said Indrani, "he will spike his dish with a cup of salt and leave no doubt who the judge is to choose."

Bhagyashree said, "If I were a cobra, I would spit on this dessert."

Tanvi said, "If I were a tiger, I would pee on this dessert."

Ishaan said, "If I were an elephant, I would trample this dessert."

Bhagyashree forgot herself and said, "Ishaan, dear, this is no time for comedy."

Indeed, it was not. Pooja burst into the room screaming, "Catastrophe!"

The others assumed reference to *poodle boy*, but they were mistaken. Pooja proceeded to stammer some kind of weather report that surprised no one: rain, wind and flooding.

"It's monsoon season," said Kanita.

Pooja clarified, "The bridge is out! The judge can't come!"

How unfortunate for you, thought Bhagyashree.

"What will we *do*?" said Pooja.

The parents had readied themselves to skewer Pooja like *tandoori*, to smoke out her lies and roast out a confession, but circumstances had changed.

"Well," said Kanita, "we can't cancel, now."

Said Indrani, "We must think of the children."

All the parents agreed that they, themselves, would judge the competition and that each would have one vote. Pooja suggested that the creator of each dish remain anonymous, but her guests refused. Arjun could not win on merit. He must not win by chance.

After more debate and much more dessert, Tanvi summarised the will of the group. "We will all vote by secret ballot, but we will not vote for our own child."

And then she included curious double-dealing of one particular word, "We all agree to *honour* the *honour* system."

By day's end, the competition had produced predictable results. The children appeared to learn a valuable lesson – outwardly, anyway – regarding the integrity of their parents and they also celebrated the long list of co-winners as they might an individual award.

Conversely, for the parents, the outcome of Best Cook Junior, Mumbai Edition was a bitter pill. Each felt betrayed by the hubris and duplicity of the others, as if a rug had been pulled out from under them. And each felt loss twenty kilometres deep as if a fault line in the earth had opened up beneath their feet and swallowed them whole and swept them out to sea.

LOUNGE LIZARDS
AMANDA HUGGINS

Art Mainprize is down by the slipway, perched on the edge of George Cappleman's boat, a crushed beer can ground into the sand below his dangling feet. It's late August, almost dark at eight o'clock, and a solemn promise of autumn is wrapped in the cool sea air. When he sees Billy Cappleman heading across from the cottages, Art reaches inside the coble and pulls out two more cans. He throws one to his friend and cracks open the other.

"Yer got a light, Bill? I've run out of matches."

Billy fumbles in the pocket of his Harrington jacket and takes out a cheap disposable lighter. Art pulls a cigarette from a soft pack of Camels and cups his hands around the uncertain flame. He leans back, takes another deep drag and offers the pack to Billy.

"Bit fancy for you, mate? Camels?"

"Good stuff these, kidder. Da got them off some bloke at work – duty frees from Lloret de Mar or wherever.

What's that crap yer wearing anyway?" He pinches Billy's jacket sleeve between his finger and thumb.

"It's what me mam got us from that bloke on the market."

Art rolls his eyes. "Bet it's fake then. Don't know what you want it for anyhow. That's what skinheads and mods wear – I thought we were rockers."

Billy blushes, then shrugs. "We are. It's just for knocking around down here and stuff. James Dean had one."

Art scoffs. "James la-di-da Dean now, is it? He yer new role model then?"

"Nah, not really. Did you know he was bisexual? Like Bowie."

"Never heard that before. You seem to know a lot about it? Thinking of trying it out?"

Billy's blush deepens. "Course not."

Art looks over Billy's shoulder and lifts his beer can in greeting. "Seth – come and have a brown ale. Billy here is just telling me how he's thinking of going bisexual."

Seth grins. "That right? I always thought there was summat different about you. But then again, I thought you were sweet on wee Helen Harrison in the chippy. How's that going? I daresay you'll not get far with her wearing that jacket."

"There's nothing wrong with this chuffing jacket. Stop going on about it, the pair of you. There's far worse sartorial choices made round here. I know someone who wears white loafers with gold chains across 'em."

Seth splutters into his beer. "What the crap does

'sartorial' mean when it's at home? And who the bloody hell wears white shoes in this village?"

Billy points at Art. "His da, that's who."

Art scowls. "And? What if he does? My old fella is cool as a Mivvi."

Billy laughs. "My da says men who wear shoes like that are lounge lizards."

"Well, we don't have a lounge, so he can't be."

"Ha ha, very funny. Well, he wears turtlenecks too, and a cravat, so…" Billy tails off, knows he's probably gone far enough.

"No, he bloody doesn't. You're just mad because your da stinks of fish."

Billy lunges forward and shoves Art in the chest. "Better than working in the shite steelworks with a set of losers."

Brown ale slops out of both beer cans and down the front of Billy's jacket. Art teeters on the edge of the coble for a second but manages to right himself.

"The truth always hurts, eh, Billy? Push me like that again and I might have to tell you summat I was hoping to spare you from."

Art slides off the edge of the boat and drops to the ground, starts walking away up the slope towards the cottages.

"Wait!" Billy runs after him. "What do you mean, 'summat you were hoping to spare me from'?"

Art shakes his head. "Nothing, Billy, nothing. I was just winding you up. I'll see yer tomorrow for the fishing."

Art lies awake for what feels like hours. There's a full moon staring straight through the thin curtains, and the dog is restless at his feet, her quivering paws running in the air as she sleeps. He feels guilty about what he said to Billy as they parted, knows he'll probably be wondering about it now. But Art still thinks it would be right to tell him; if he was Billy, he'd want to know the rumours about his mam and her fancy man. They're saying she goes into town on the bus, drinking in the Crown with some slick fella – the type of bloke her husband would call a lounge lizard if he wasn't too busy on the trawlers to think about it. It makes him sick to think of Billy's mam with some slime ball like that. And what if she ups and goes – walks out of her job at the factory and leaves poor George to look after Billy and his sister? Billy might be fifteen now, but his kid sister is only eight, and George works long hours out on the trawlers as well as taking out his own coble.

He finally drifts off, only to wake with a start when he hears a key in the door beneath his window. He looks at the glowing red digits of his alarm clock and sees it's well after two. Where the bloody hell has his da been until now? He hears Mam open the parlour door, realises she's been waiting up. She was supposed to be away over at her sister's tonight, but she must have changed her mind and come back. He can hear urgent muttering just inside the porch, heavy footsteps going down the passageway to the kitchen, then the sliding door closes with a rattle.

Art creeps along the landing. He can hear his father's

voice, calm and measured, his mam's voice choked up with anger and tears. He can't make out their words, but then the kitchen door slides back again and his da marches down the hall and out of the front door. His mam stands in the porch and shouts after him.

"You haven't been in't Dolphin until this time, Shaun Mainprize – in fact you haven't been in there at all."

"I–"

"No, save yer breath, I went down to check. And you still haven't told me why you're wearing your best clobber on a Tuesday night?"

Art slips back into his room, looks out of the window, watches his da standing in the street, hands on hips. He's wearing a patterned shirt with a long, pointed collar, some kind of cream blazer, and on his feet are a pair of white loafers, the gold chains glinting in the moonlight.

The following day is bright and warm, the sky a barefaced blue, and just before midday Art meets up with Billy by the slipway. George has asked Billy to take the boat out and check the lobster pots, and they've both brought sandwiches as well as their fishing gear.

Art jumps off the sea wall and looks Billy up and down. "I see you're still wearing that crap jacket, yer lounge lizard."

"Will you ever shut up about it?" He shrugs off the Harrington and folds it up. "Too hot for it anyway."

Art follows his lead, takes off his denim jacket, and Billy reaches out to pull at the V-neck of his jumper.

"Lounge lizard yerself, you look like a Bay City Roller in that thing."

"You're the lounge lizard, kidder."

"No, you are. You're the king of lounge lizards!"

They give each other a friendly shove and Billy stumbles over a coil of rope. Art laughs and Billy laughs with him. He feels warm inside, blessed to have such a good mate, a friend he knows he can trust. Though he'll kill himself before he ever tells him.

They borrow Mousey's tractor to launch the coble, and after checking and rebaiting the empty pots, they set up two rods and lie back in the boat, heads resting on their folded jackets, eyes closed against the sun. They let the boat drift, neither of them talking, and Art dozes off for a while until he hears Billy's voice.

"What were yer going to tell me yesterday?"

"Eh?"

"That thing you said you were hoping to spare me from?"

"Oh, that. Nothing, kidder, I told you, I was just trying to wind you up."

"Well, if it's summat about me mam, I already know what people are saying – but it isn't true. I'd know if it was."

"Yeah, yeah, course you would, kid. I just… well, I just thought you should know the rumours. What did you do last night when you got in anyhow? I listened to the new Deep Purple cassette again – it's a blinder."

"I didn't do anything really, just watched the telly. I had to keep an eye on me sister 'cause everyone was out. Da was working on Colin Bain's boat last night – extra shift because Mousey's ill."

Art nods. "What about yer mam? Where was she last night?"

"She were working as well, until about two in the morning, I think – there's loads of overtime for the machinists right now. The shops are ordering for Christmas already, she reckons; all the women want their new parlour curtains for the big day. She's been doing a lot of extra lately."

Art nods again, as though he's mulling everything over, and Billy pauses for a moment, remembers what Seth told him that morning outside the newsagents. "Where did your da head out to last night, Art? Seth said he was seen getting out of a town taxi at two in the morning – in his lounge lizard gear. And Millie Halton is spreading some tale of yer mam shouting at him in the street."

Art doesn't answer, and the silence hangs heavy between them as something shifts and falls into place. Something they both hope isn't true, but which they understand may become true if they utter the possibility of it out loud. It's unfamiliar territory and neither of them know how to navigate it. The boat drifts on the calm water, a lone gull circles overhead, and the only sound is the gentle slosh against the side of the hull.

Eventually they both unpack their sandwiches and eat them without saying a word. When they've finished, Art passes Billy a Camel. Billy pulls out his lighter, catches Art's eye for a moment as he leans towards the flame, but still neither of them can bring themselves to speak. Afterwards, they lie back down and both feign sleep beneath the warm afternoon sun. Out of the corner of his eye, Art is sure he sees Billy scratch his nose, but he remains quiet and maintains the charade, doesn't ask the questions which are tumbling around in his head.

Like, where will everyone live if Billy's mam goes off with his da? Maybe they can all muck in together – Art and his mam sharing the house with Billy, his da and his sister. Art and Billy could have the big attic room and Mam could look after them all. He likes Billy's da; he always learns a lot when he goes out on the boat with him. In fact, maybe George will find him a job on the trawlers and he won't have to follow his own da into the steelworks – he'll tell him to stuff it where the sun don't shine, along with his stupid white loafers.

When Art finally sits up, he realises they've drifted too far out, that they have almost reached the next headland. From this new vantage point everything looks different – the cottages are hidden by the pier and the long beach is a mere sliver of silver. It's an unfamiliar place, seen for the very first time, a town unravelled and sea-changed. It is a place which felt safe and solid when they left it behind that morning, yet now it appears unsure of itself, slightly unreal, as though a strong gust of wind could carry it away.

THE LADY VICAR
PHOEBE HURST

The church has a new vicar. A lady vicar. I saw her in the post office last Wednesday. She walked with a stoop and her knuckles were large and surprisingly scuffed for a lady but that was what she was, a lady vicar. She had the black clerical shirt and collar around her neck, flat-soled shoes suitable for long hours spent preaching on the feet. There was no mistaking what she was.

I stood in line to buy a second-class stamp. The man in front quibbled about an envelope so there was time to watch her, the Lady Vicar. The way she moved was broad and comical. She spun the rack with the greetings cards until it squeaked and swayed. In her arms she had a pair of curtains. They dragged on the floor like some awful dead thing. Ah, but then I understood. Of course, these weren't curtains but her vicar's robes. Her Lady Vicar's robes.

Behind me was old Mrs Tilney and her lips thinned when she saw this. No way for a vicar to behave, she was thinking. What with her being a lady in the first place and then here she is handling consecrated vestments like yesterday's dirty socks. She tutted but the Lady Vicar was burrowing between the chocolate digestives and showed no sign of having heard.

The post office owner called over, "Can I help you?"

The Lady Vicar looked up, startled.

"Terribly sorry," she said, and when she did so, I realised that she had what is referred to as a 'sing-song' voice. She 'trilled' in a 'sing-song' voice, you might have said. Me, I'm not one for singing – or speaking, for that matter. I much prefer to listen than talk, least of all in a musical manner. But I believe I am right in describing her to you as a Lady Vicar with a sing-song voice.

"Terribly sorry," she said. "Could you tell me where the Strepsils are?"

"Strepsils," the post office owner said.

"Or any other brand of throat lozenge. I'm not picky."

The post office owner showed her to where they keep the toothpaste and boxes of aspirin. The man with his envelope huffed and puffed, Mrs Tilney tutted. Me, I'm not an impatient man. Give me an hour and I'll wait it. I'll wait two if necessary. Three, four, seven. It's not time that scares me, it's the things people fill it with. And so I waited while the Lady Vicar selected a packet of cherry-flavoured throat lozenges. Her robes were grey and worn at the elbows. Being a Lady Vicar, she would know how to prepare a boil wash and make the necessary needle repairs. That's what I assumed, anyway.

The post office owner held the door for the Lady Vicar as she left, ignoring the man with his envelope and Mrs Tilney's narrowed mouth. She took the owner's hand between her large knuckles and thanked him, then turned to us in the queue.

"Peace be with you," she trilled in a sing-song voice. "Peace be with each of you."

Of course, I had no problem with her. A Lady Vicar dragging her robes around the post office on a Wednesday afternoon. I'm not a religious man.

•

You can call me Bean, everyone else does. This is not because I bear any resemblance to Mr Bean, the character in the television programme, but because I don't speak much. In fact, he and I couldn't be more different if we tried – physically, I mean. But I would have to agree with people that we are both men of few words.

Over the years I have developed gestures to communicate my needs. In the pharmacy, where I go every Wednesday after the post office, I interact with the girl by pointing first to myself and then the medication stacked on shelves behind her. She smiles and makes a comment about the weather or the new bench on the village green, already defaced by one of the Barry lads, though she knows not to expect a reply. A nice girl, that one, and I make sure to tip my hat to her on the way out. (This is another gesture I have developed.)

It wasn't like this when the Sister was around. She spoke for both of us, I never even had to think about opening my mouth. I suppose that's how I came by the habit of not talking. When someone speaks on your behalf, you don't need to learn the words.

•

I watched a film with him in once. Mr Bean. He works at the National Gallery and is sent by his employer to an art gallery in Los Angeles. The Americans think they're getting an esteemed professor of art but in fact Mr Bean is a nuisance gallery attendant and the Brits are glad to be rid of him. So the supposed Dr Bean stays with an unsuspecting American and his family and is tasked with looking after a famous painting – I don't remember which – and of course he gets into all sorts of trouble and ruins the painting, but it's alright because the family decide that they love this odd British man who doesn't speak and embrace him as one of their own.

I don't remember how it ends, but that's the general gist.

•

I do remember one thing. The American asks Mr Bean about his work at the London gallery. This is before he finds out that he is a fraud. But Mr Bean answers honestly, I suppose because he knows no other way. He says,

"My job is to sit and look at paintings." That's it. Nothing else. The American, he goes wild for this. "You just sit and look," he says, all excitable. If only more academics took the time to simply sit and look at the great works of art they study! The joke is that the American has confused the labour of a low-skilled gallery attendant with that of a decorated art historian.

It's not a funny joke. Sitting and looking seems a very noble thing to me.

•

Don't mind him, the Sister used to say. We're together.

•

Strangely enough, I do sit and look at paintings. Well, not paintings, picture postcards of paintings. The Sister, since she left the village, has become a sort of collector. Each time she visits an art gallery and sees a painting she likes, she buys a postcard and sends it to me. There must be a great number of art galleries in the place where she lives now because I have over one hundred postcards. I fix each one to the kitchen wall with masking tape. The effect really is quite impressive. And yes, of an evening, after the tea things have been cleared, I sit in front of the wall and I look.

I look at the ripening fruit arranged in pools of light. I look at the landscapes of sea and sky and mountain, grazing cattle and bailed hay. I look at the abstract art with its oil splatters and blocks of colour. I look at the courtly men in powdered wigs, the long dead queens fingering their pearls.

Other times, I focus on a single painting. Take this one, for example, which shows three people in a forest. They sit next to an upturned basket. Cherries and bread spill across the grass. It is two men and a lady. One of the men leans back and motions with his hand as if emphasising a point. The other stares off into the middle distance, ignoring whatever his friend has to say.

And then the lady.

The lady is naked. Stark naked, not a scrap of clothing on her. The men wear pressed shirts and neat trouser creases, one of them has a pocket watch. The lady wears nothing. Her skin is so pale and fleshy against the dark trees that the contrast is almost painful. It is painful. A naked lady between two clothed men, her hat and clothes tossed to the floor. Looking at the painting makes me very uneasy.

But what might be more painful, more uneasy, is the way the naked lady stares you right in the eye. Nakedness is not embarrassing to her.

•

There are no art galleries in the village. Only a post office, a pharmacy, a bus stop and a new bench on the green, already spoiled by graffiti.

•

The funny thing about sitting and looking at paintings, or picture postcards of paintings, is that they change the longer you do it. After a while, I realise who the naked lady reminds me of. It's the way she rests her chin on her hand. She is the Lady Vicar.

•

The following Wednesday, it rains and rains. The bus stop is next to a dip in the road and if you have lived here for years like I have, you know to stay well back. But the Lady Vicar is new and does not know this. She stands on the kerb as three of the older Barry boys, no doubt playing truant, tear through the puddle on their bikes and drench her from head to foot. The boys pedal off, having the cheek to laugh as they do so. A terrible family that, wrong'uns, the whole lot of them. The Lady Vicar stands there, wiping water from her eyes. Then she looks up and sees me. She smiles, cold and wet and ridiculed.

"Good for the garden," she says. "All this rain."

•

I don't know how to reply to the postcards. I buy stamps at the post office but the words won't come. The irony is that the Sister would know what to say. If I could just get the Sister to write a reply to her own postcard then the problem would be solved. She talks for England, people said about the Sister. The brother – me, they'd be referring to, she was the Sister and I was the Brother – is quiet as the grave but that woman has a voice on her and knows how to use it.

•

I go to see the Lady Vicar in action. Sunday morning at the village church. There aren't many in the congregation. A few families from the school, old Mrs Tilney, one or two I don't recognise. During the first hymn, a lady comes and takes the children for Sunday school so that leaves even less of us. The Lady Vicar doesn't mind. When she stands in the light of the stained-glass window, you hardly notice her robes' frayed hems.

It's a long time since I attended church and I have forgotten a few of the particulars. At the door, I'm given a hymn book and a service sheet. The way the service sheet works is that there are words in plain text when the vicar – or Lady Vicar in our case – speaks, followed by words in bold when the congregation joins in. To give you an example:

The Lord be with you
And with thy spirit.
Lift up your hearts.
We lift them up unto the Lord.
Let us give thanks unto the Lord our God.
It is right to give thanks and praise.

I don't join in but I listen very carefully. I hear the Lady Vicar's sing-song voice, then the chorus of response. When it is the congregation's turn to speak, she recites the words along with them so that by the end of the service, she has said every word in the service sheet, plain and bold. It's a lot of words, far more than I have spoken in years.

At the end of the service, I wait for everyone else to leave. I look down at my feet, not wanting to get them in a muddle as I step down from the pew. The Lady Vicar approaches. She doesn't offer an arm or anything so silly, but stands nearby in case I had wanted to steady myself. She would be a good person to steady yourself on, being as broad as she is.

"Perhaps you'd like to come to my study for a cup of tea," she says.

•

There is another lady in the painting. In the background, paddling with undergarments hitched to her knees. I try not to worry about her like I worry about the lady with no clothes. She has made her choice, she is somewhere else. I must accept this.

•

I have never been in a normal vicar's study so I can't tell you the difference between that such room and the one belonging to the Lady Vicar. Something I can say is that there are a lot of books. Books in cardboard boxes, books on shelves from floor to ceiling, books on the desk and in piles by the French windows that open onto a lawn with fuzzy thickets of dandelion. Most are theological, but I spot a few pink covers and titles that refer to shopping, romance and shoes. They are the kind of books that the Sister borrowed from the mobile library, when she lived in the village. Books for ladies.

The Lady Vicar tells me to make myself comfortable in an armchair. She brings the tea and offers shortbread from a tin. She takes a large piece for herself and when she has finished eating, she wipes her mouth on the back of her hand. Before I know what's happening, I am leaning over my knees. I haven't touched my shortbread but my throat is dry and prickly. I look at the Lady Vicar's face and I speak.

"What is it like to be a lady vicar?"

She thinks for a moment.

"Having never been a man vicar, I've nothing to compare it to."

I have to look away then. She doesn't mind and seems to enjoy the breeze from the garden. I start panting. My mouth gapes like a dog in the sun but I make myself do it again.

"Where are the words from? The ones you say in church."

The Lady Vicar goes to the shelf and takes down a hardcover book.

"This is the Book of Common Prayer," she says, opening at a page near the back. "Look here, the First Sunday after the Epiphany. This was our service today. People have recited these words for generations."

The pages are very thin, like tissue, and print bleeds through from the reverse.

"I don't like to speak," I say. "This is a rare occurrence, what we are doing now. It was the Sister who was the talker. Me, I like to sit and look."

I try to give the book back but the Lady Vicar presses it into my hands.

"It's nice when someone else has thought of the words for you," she says.

"Yes."

"And the Sister, is she…"

"Gone."

The Lady Vicar smiles. Suddenly I feel grateful and wish that I could give a signal of thanks but I have removed my hat and silent gestures seem silly now that I am here, speaking far more than I have in years.

"You must have nothing but words," I say. "Words for couples and new babies, school assemblies and grieving widows. Words, words, words. And then the ones in that book. The dear lord and the amen. Peace be with you and lift up your hearts."

The Lady Vicar stands and closes the French windows, making the room airless.

"At the end of a busy Sunday, I have spoken so much and to so many people that my throat burns and I hear a ringing in my ears," she says. "I wear out my voice speaking someone else's words."

She grips the door handle and her large knuckles turn white.

"Then why do you do it?"

"Because they are God's words and I'm glad to speak them," she says. "It is right to give thanks and praise."

The prayer book drops to the floor.

"And if your god is gone," I say, my voice barely a whisper. "If the god who created the words you relied on your whole life goes, leaving you with nothing but silence, what do you do?"

The Lady Vicar lets go of the door and walks to where the book fell from my hands. She picks it up and smooths the pages, then places it gently in my lap.

"But that's the best thing," she says. "God's words are never gone. They're always there. You need only to open your mouth and they will come."

•

That evening, after the tea things have been cleared, I turn my back to the postcards. The Lady Vicar's copy of the Book of Common Prayer is dog-eared from use, spine cracked, but it serves my purpose. I open at the first page and do not stop until I have spoken every word. Plain and bold, priest and congregation, dear lord and amen. Words, words, words. The words that destroy the Lady Vicar's throat but make her defiant when naked, unafraid.

Head resting on fat and placid knuckles, so sure of her god. I sharpen my pencil and arrange the envelope and the second-class stamp. I draw the writing paper towards me. To the Sister, I write. I am sorry that it has taken so long.

YOUR COMMUNITY NOTICEBOARD
RACHEL PATTINSON

It's about three-quarters of the way between Mrs Foster's classroom and the toilets. A sign at the top says YOUR COMMUNITY NOTICEBOARD. The idea is that if anyone has a poster to put up, this is the place. Except nobody does, so the adverts are for concerts that were years ago and there's an old wellbeing sign that's starting to go yellow.

The community noticeboard and I are similar, in some ways. Mostly empty, and we don't say very much. In fact, people usually just look past us.

But this week there's something different about the community noticeboard. A sheet of white A4, which says in bold letters:

CLAP DURING ASSEMBLY WHILE MISS TAYLOR IS TALKING

That's all. Nothing else. No link to go to for more information. No explanation. And I'm not going to ask anyone about it, obviously.

I'd almost forgotten I'd seen it until I walked into the school hall. Miss Taylor's sitting at the back of the stage, which means she must be part of the assembly. When she gets up to speak, I have this prickly feeling at the back of my throat. I remember the sign. I know I'm going to look pretty sad, but that's nothing new. So, I do it anyway, just to see what happens. I clap, and even add a little thumbs up at the end for good measure.

"Thank you for your enthusiasm, Dylan." Miss Taylor looks delighted that I've voluntarily communicated. She must think I'm really excited about the extra GCSE revision sessions she's organising.

Jasmine, who's sitting next to me, nudges me with her elbow and smiles at me sideways. "What was that about?"

I don't say anything, but I grin back at her.

Another day, another sign. On Tuesday it says:

WEAR YOUR JUMPER BACK TO FRONT
FOR THE REST OF THE DAY

I stop. I take off my jumper, turn it over and put it back on again. It's clearly not the way it's designed to be worn, so it's kind of uncomfortable around my neck. I feel a bit disorientated throughout English. I keep wanting to twist my head to find the right opening. Quite a few people point it out.

"Dylan, mate, why is your jumper the wrong way round?" Harry asks.

Because the community noticeboard told me to. I can't really explain, like normal, so I just shrug.

Harry gives a shrug back. "Fair enough."

I'm not sure I ever made a conscious decision to stop talking. To Harry, who's been my friend since forever, and everyone else. It's not that I don't talk at all. When teachers speak to me directly, I'll answer. And when I need something, I'll ask. But apart from that, I find silence easier.

It started a couple of months ago. People kept encouraging me to talk about what was going on and how I was feeling. But I didn't know what to say. I couldn't find the words. And then I kind of stopped trying to find any of them.

After a couple of weeks Miss Taylor brought my parents in, and made me sit there while they all talked around me. I sort of went along with it and said 'yes' and 'no' when I felt like I had to. They concluded I'd probably start talking again when I was ready, and I nodded because I just wanted the meeting to be over.

I think other people at school found it weird to begin with, but now most of Year 10 have accepted it and given up. Thankfully not Harry or Jasmine though, who still include me in conversations like I'm taking part in them.

As I walk past the community noticeboard again today, I'm wondering what it will say next, and why nobody else seems to be noticing it.

SKIP OUT OF MATHS AND COME BACK HERE

In maths, I feel like I'm in the wrong place. The noticeboard is where I need to be. It's not that difficult to get out. I wait until about halfway through Mr Kaur's lesson on calculating the volume of a cylinder, then I catch him and indicate I need to leave the class to go to the toilet. As I walk towards that same familiar corridor, I wonder what I'm going to find.

And when I get to the community noticeboard, Jasmine and Harry are there, standing next to it. They must have skipped out of fourth period too. They are smiling and bundle me into a hug. I read a new notice over Jasmine's shoulder:

WE WILL ALWAYS BE YOUR COMMUNITY

"We don't need you to talk, Dylan," Harry says, his forehead close to mine. "We've been friends since Year 2, remember?"

"But we're here whenever you're ready to," Jasmine adds. "Even if you want us to keep sending you messages like this."

I hug them back. Maybe I can try to start responding to them, and not just to anonymous signs on the community noticeboard.

"Okay," I whisper.

ARRIETA EINSTEIN
BRYAN PEARSON

I've just stuck a pill in my mouth and drunk the water quickly because the saccharin traditionally used to mask the taste has long since run out. In fact, the ninety-year war with the Asiatic-Chindian-Contingent has caused just about everything to run out.

From the window, my eyes follow the path of the luminous yellow smoke as it billows out its message to the masses. The Primo-Gathering imposed dye, added to the smoke, tells all that behold it that it's saturated with carcinogens. Stepping out in the city during such furnace evacuations is suicide without the alveoli pill. There'll be a fifteen-minute wait until my lungs are infused with the vaccine. The feeling's not unpleasant. I, for one, get a warm glow all over.

Out of the lift and into the street I walk, holding my can of coma-mace up my sleeve – ready to spray at the slightest of incidents. Those poor homogenous souls condemned to wander the old roads with their mouths stitched shut, each of them now a vessel for The Edible Cyst Programme.

'Let's grow food on their heads,' came the cry from the Primo-Gathering and there was no going back. The worst part is the use of the straightjackets to stop them interfering with the harvest. With their tongues gone and sexual identities removed, they trudge the concrete farmways of Upper-Manhattan until their bounty all but tips them over. Their only crime: Primo-Verbal-Disputo. As usual, the pathetic forms pose no threat on my short journey through their domain. The coma-mace is slipped back from sleeve to femur pouch before entering the code for the door.

The music hits me and the corners of my mouth curl up as they do every time I enter the building. The smile turns into fully blown singing as the nursery rhyme reaches it chorus.

"Morning, Arrietta," says Charlie, the door-watch.

I only manage a wave as usual, walking by him, because the implant in my chest makes me sing two choruses of the song. Apparently, it's soothing to the foetuses and promotes early growth.

"Morning, Miss Einstein." Crawley, the corridor runner, greets me with a tray of microchips.

"Morning, Crawley. How's your arse for warts?"

"Yeh, very funny. These chips are all back from Regains. Doc says can you scrub 'em, debug 'em and stick 'em up someone else's ar–"

"Yeh, I know where to stick 'em, Crawley. Now bugger off back down that corridor before I put a straitjacket on you."

"Keep your genetically modified hair on, Moon-pants," he says.

I chuckle after Crawley. The decision has been a long time coming, but I made my mind up a week or so ago. As soon as my Primo-Maternal-Cycle-Period is over. As soon as I've got shot of this eighth and final batch, I'm having one of my own. And when the time comes, I want Crawley to be the donor. I will have his secretion commandeered from the medi-board if I must. When I was given my Medico-Surgical-Enhancement-Menu at the outset: any three of a choice of seven to go with the three mandatory ones they said. My first choice was 'The Bitch Chip'. I read in the literature that it enhances women's natural maternal and self-preservation instinct. I can only concur that it works. Having said that, I do think Crawley will give up his treasure freely. I've watched him observe my second menu choice daily. The mammary extensions, chosen for their capacity for milk, have other advantages. I intend to ask him nearer the time anyway.

The conveyor jolts, signalling an infant chip session is about to start. The overhead halogens intensify automatically until the place is saturated with white light. The chipping rod swings down from the hub above my head – closely followed by the fry an' freeze stick. Any second now the cot-line will reach me, so I tip out the chips, delivered by Crawley, on to the table in front of me. A quick zap each with the fry an' freeze stick takes the chips from minus two-hundred- and seventy-three-degrees Celsius right through to three-hundred and seventy-two. Even the septebolaaids virus perishes in those range extremities. The cots approach. The chipping rod emits its high-pitched squeal.

Doc walks in. "Arrietta darling." He hugs me. "Check out the first twelve. These are the ones I fed with the new alpha-protein." The cot-line comes to a stop at the barrier. Doc leads me over to the first and pushes down the hood. "Look!" In his excitement, he rushes from cot to cot pushing down the hoods.

"Wow." I notice immediately what Doc is excited about. Yet the full impact isn't apparent until I eye up the contents of cots thirteen to twenty-four. These two dozen babes are my last batch. They were all born on the same day: the second of May – three weeks ago. "Jesus H. Christ on horseback, Doc, they're the size of two-year-olds."

"Not far off. Physically they're the equivalent of thirty-two months."

"What about the others?"

"As I expected. They're the equivalent of twenty-four months as usual."

"So, the new superfecundation initiative hasn't worked."

"On the contrary. The multiple-donor-program wasn't about acceleration. It was about identification. Take a closer look. The first twelve are identical duodecaplets. The second are each as different as snowflakes."

Doc is right. Looking at the second dozen again, it's

easy to spot the differences. Wait! What's with number twenty-one?

The heat in the chipping chamber feels oppressive. Twenty one's eyes are softer. Is it the light? So vulnerable. I move closer to take the babe from the cot. Almost floating, my arms outstretch.

"Arrietta!" shouts Doc.

The melting feeling that had engulfed me disappears with Doc's raised voice.

"Start from this end, Arrietta darling."

"But, Doc, I–"

"Fetch the chipping rod. It won't stop squealing until it's completed its programmed sequence. You know the script – every chip must reach thirty-seven degrees." His voice was insistent, raised perhaps an octave higher, just sufficient to defy defiance and for the first time during my Materno-Cycle, I find myself internally questioning the whole sequence. Doc wanders over to the window, his hands held behind his back.

The handle of the rod is unusually clumsy in my grip as I stumble along from cot to cot trying to regain control of my thoughts. The image of the babe in cot twenty-one is all-consuming. As the rod goes in and out, time after time. The cosy whirring of the self-guiding mechanism numbs me until the acceptance bleep reminds me that I'm getting further down the line.

"Of course, you do realise that the second twelve are destined for greatness." Doc turns away from the window as he speaks.

"Sorry, Doc, I missed that." I heard his voice, yet the words escaped me. All I can concentrate on is the cot fourth from the end. The one I will reach – next but two.

"The first twelve are just meat – cannon fodder if you will. They'll be bigger and stronger than any other troops that we've ever sent to The Greater War of Attrition. They'll be marching off, fully-grown, to fight in twenty-one weeks."

My mouth goes dry. I have never stopped to think of doing the math. A quick calculation in my head confirms Doc's statement. "But what of the second twelve? You say they are destined for greatness." The fourth cot from the end appears in front of me. I gaze down at the babe. Its eyes open and it looks up at me. The mouth moves. Is that a smile?

Doc turns back to the window. "They'll be officers! They'll be trained in the art of war. They will lead the biggest assault on the A.C.C. for fifty-six years."

I'm going through the motions now. My fingers fumble at the swaddling, the babe burps and chuckles. It definitely smiles this time. The bare pink flesh is exposed. My God, the babe is a girl child. A quick look to the side tells me Doc is occupied and the decision is made instantly. The rod vibrates quite pleasantly in my mouth, but I gag as the self-guiding mechanism slithers down my throat. The urge to vomit overwhelms me. Holding my breath, I pray for an acceptance bleep. Will the chip know it's in the wrong host?

"Come on, Arrietta. Let's get a move on."

I turn to look at Doc. He still faces the window.

BLEEP.

Doc turns as I sit the rod on the conveyer. "Hells bells! You took your time with twenty-one, didn't you?"

"Sorry, Doc. It's a girl-child. It threw me a bit. It's the first one for me." I hurry back into action on number twenty-two.

"It's the first one – period – since I started farming soldiers fifty years ago."

"How has that happened then, Doc?"

"Multiple-donor-program."

"So, it was just nature taking its course."

"There's nothing natural about the multi-donor-program, Arrietta darling. The donor sperm in each case was treated with the DNA from some very famous people. In fact, your womb has played host to the DNA of some of history's most successful military commanders."

I feel a little nauseous at Doc's latest revelation and when the last cot is dealt with, the rod stops squealing and the conveyer starts creaking back to the nursery, I feel compelled to ask the question. "Just whose DNA, exactly, has been growing in me?"

"With my connections, Arrietta darling, nothing is impossible. Government archaeology teams are looking for more as we speak. It's rumoured that the A.C.C. have found the remains of Genghis Khan and are at present diverting a river in the hunt for Attila the Hun."

"My God, Doc! Please! Who?"

"Well, we started with recent known burial sites.

Number thirteen is General Norman Schwarzkopf. The grave was only three-hundred years old. Fourteen is Hannibal Barca. He was the most ambitious. I have high hopes for him."

"Jesus, Doc–"

"No, we couldn't find him. God knows we looked."

"No! I mean Jesus, Doc. Who the hell else's DNA has been floating around in me?"

"I wanted Julius Caesar, but apparently the bastards cremated him. Obviously, there's Hitler and Napoleon – deluded maniacs of course, but we need the military genius."

"Jesus, Doc. You filled my fucking belly full of dead dictator DNA. You can't do that."

"I think you'll find I can, and I did, and I will be doing it again shortly."

"Oh no, you won't, Doc. My internship is up after this lot. I'm having one of my own next."

"Arrietta darling, your womb and everything else belongs to me."

"But I was promised." Tears come out so fast I can hear them.

"Yes. We do say that to keep you all focused. But, actually, at this point, we give you a choice of carrying on with the program or getting shipped out to Coney Island. We've got an edible cyst farm there specially for Materno-Usurpers." Doc brushes the top of my head. "A good strong cranium you've got there, Arrietta darling. It should hold up a stone or two between trimmings."

'Trimmings' is the last word Doc says because the chipping rod smashes through his teeth and destroys his brain. I rifle through his pockets because of no other reason than I've seen them do it in the century's old DVDs we Materno-Mothers watch for hours and hours. Now I know why they do it. I've found a list. It's numbered from thirteen to twenty-four. I'm getting out of this shit hole. I'm running down to the nursery now – my heart fit to burst. I've heard it's the size of an aerodrome, but I know when I get there, I'll find my sweet Boadicea.

MURDO LIVAN
PAM PLUMB

The ferry shivers as it nestles against the harbour wall. Whitewashed, the town of Brean looks cold against the darkening sky. Beyond the port, the headland rolls out in gloomy undulations that hunch into the darkening horizon. Fortune Ngubu braces herself against the wind and watches the other passengers gather their belongings. Busy parents marshal their children, urging them not to stare in her direction. A rowdy set of Americans, who had generously shared their every thought during the crossing, barrel towards the exit.

Like most of her jobs, she expects this one to be short lived. Three days at most. Just a few sketchy details of the post had been proffered in the email. Fortune wouldn't have pursued it but something about the location intrigued her. And it was more than her standard fee so there'd been no reason to turn it down.

All of the road signs are in Gaelic and English but Fortune ignores them, preferring to follow the directions she'd been sent. Twenty minutes to get to the hotel once she passes the golf course and then takes a left. As she drives through the barren landscape, the wind nudging the car, Fortune thinks about her new employer. Of course she'd googled him, but it had thrown up nothing. No social media accounts, no images. Nothing. It was as though he'd been manufactured just for the purpose of this appointment.

A light mist has developed and in the darkness Fortune nearly misses the golf club. The hire car's brakes squeal as she skids into the left hand turn. *Slow down, girl. There's no rush.* She wasn't ready for a dunking in the lochs that ran alongside the tarmac. She passes no one as she continues on the narrow road. The instructions are accurate. Fortune steps through the door of the hotel bar exactly twenty minutes after leaving Brean, but she feels that during the journey Time has chewed her up and spat her out fifty years earlier. Small wall lights sluice the room. Slouching regulars line the bar, turning as one many-headed beast to eye the newcomer. She gauges the room. No women. No children. Seven men, including the barman and an old dog that whines at the feet of his owner who is smoking a pipe. *A lawless place. Watch yourself, girl.*

"I've a room booked under the name of Mitchell."

The barman hesitates a moment. Then nods, wiping his hands on his shirt as he rounds the bar. "The room's ready if you want to go straight up."

"Murdo Livan, do you know him?"

A couple of the men at the bar shift on their stools. It is a moment before the barman speaks. "He hasn't been around for a long time."

"He contacted me last week. We have arranged to meet."

The barman glances at the pipe smoker, then takes Fortune's bag.

"I'll show you to your room." Fortune follows the barman when the old smoker says. "You'll find his house next to the old chapel on the Fisk road."

Fortune musters a smile. "Thank you. I'll take a look in the morning."

The mist has turned to mizzle, thickening the night. Reluctant to wait till the morning she has driven up to the house next to the chapel. It is hard to get a full picture in the shifting shards of light as she pans its facade with her torch but the house looks rundown. The door is open, swaying drunkenly in the wind. No hint of occupation. She steps inside, scanning the first room. The ceiling is coming in, furniture is in disarray, personal belongings scattered as though abandoned in an earthquake. A frameless photograph, bent almost to the point of dissection, sits on the mantelpiece. Next to it is an old bird's nest, splatters of guano decorating the hearth in place of a rug. Fortune steps further into the room, feeling like she is trespassing, though the broken walls and discarded gubbins tell her that Murdo Livan hasn't been here for a good while.

She jumps as a startled bird arrows past her and out the open door. Gently stepping over old fashioned crockery and blackened cooking pots, Fortune reaches for the photograph. It feels dry in her hand despite the rain coming in through the roof. Dislodged muck blanches her fingers. The man in the photograph is dressed in a suit from the 60s. Tailored, clipped, black. In the background is a low-roofed house that might be this house. She turns it over. In the torch light she reads the faded ink: Murdo – Sept 21st 1963. She flips the photo back and trains the torch light onto the image. Is this the same Murdo that had employed her? If it was, Fortune was surprised; she'd imagined him to be younger. It wasn't so much that he was familiar with technology – more the language he'd used was modern, not the words of an older man. But why send her to this wreck of a place, to an address that was no longer in use?

She thought back to the hotel barman. Perhaps this dereliction explained his wariness. But why not just tell her the place was abandoned? Why let her go through this charade? With a sigh Fortune scans the remainder of the room. Nothing. Nothing of interest anyway. She places the photo in her pocket and turns to leave. At the threshold she snaps off her torch; someone else is here. She reaches for the Luger holstered under her right arm.

From the doorway she watches a strong beam of light interrogate her car. Fortune follows the beam to its source but its owner is cloaked in darkness, the swirling mist making visibility poor. Hearing footsteps crunch closer, the visitor's torch light bobbing in time with each step, she goes further back into the shelter of the house, wanting to watch but not be seen. She is ready. The Luger rests in her left hand, index finger hooked in the curve of the trigger. She waits. One more step, one more bob of torch light. The beam enters the house, seems to search for her. Fortune controls her breathing, waits for the attack.

Then the light goes out. She blinks white dots away. The darkness is absolute. Over the sound of the wind Fortune listens for movement, still poised with the Luger. Hears nothing save her own shallow breathing and the ache of the wind. She waits. A lost tourist would have come into the house for shelter. So is it one of the drinkers from the bar, come to check her out? Or is it Murdo Livan? She knows so little of him. For all she knows he could have brought her here, set her up for something. She curses under her breath for letting herself get caught in this position. *Most unprofessional, Fortune.*

She maintains her position for two whole minutes, her shoulder muscles beginning to complain. *You'll have to make the move, girl.* She clicks off the safety catch, steps forward.

"Who's there?" She snaps on the torch, hoping to blind her challenger for a moment, giving her time to assess the danger. She sweeps the beam in a wide arc from left to right, right to left, passing over the car and the gravel path, over to the road and beyond. *Where are they?* She hasn't heard footsteps or a car leaving. Fortune scans again. The rain is heavier, the mist swirling into white globs of fog. *Get out of here.* She holsters the Luger and jumps in the car, an unfamiliar feeling of fear skittering through her well-covered bones.

As soon as Fortune steps through the door, the barman looks at her, a complicated expression on his face. She can't decide if he is relieved or disappointed that she has returned. The other men, the same ones that littered the bar before, stop their chatter and stare at her without embarrassment. They too seem a bit taken aback to see her. The old smoker is gone, though his dog remains, his chin on his paws, eyebrows twitching as he surveys the situation.

"You found Murdo, then?"

Fortune considers the question. He'd told her Murdo Livan had not been seen lately so why would he expect her to have met him? She smiles again but says nothing.

In the morning Fortune ponders her next move. The email she'd received from Murdo Livan had been explicit: to meet him at that address where he would explain her task. So why would he send her to that derelict place? Had he planted that photo as some strange clue? Fortune chuckles lightly to herself. *This isn't your usual job, now, is it, girl?* Despite her laughter, she is frustrated too. Yes, her trip had been paid for and most of her fee was already in the bank. She could legitimately return home today knowing she'd been at the rendezvous, even if her client had not. But no. She'd been hired to do a job and she intended to see it through.

Overnight, the mist had curled itself back over the edges of the hills, leaving the road and surrounding lochs clear and bright. A strong September wind steals the warmth of the sunshine. Fortune arrives at the gravel driveway of the derelict house again. In the daylight she sees what could only be sensed in the misty darkness of last night, the truly deplorable state of the place. At first glance it seems to have been abandoned decades ago, but then Fortune spots some modern features: electrical wiring, a telephone point and an oil storage unit squatting at the side of the building.

She skirts round the back of the house, picking her way through thistles and charred pieces of timber. Half hidden in the overgrown disorder is a metal shed, its roof pockmarked with rust, its door half open. Anyone would think it as derelict and forsaken as the house but Fortune pauses at the sight of a shiny new padlock, dangling unhinged, swaying in the breeze. She smiles to herself, remembering her jitters last night. Was this where the mysterious visitor had disappeared to? Or perhaps this was Mr Livan's new abode? A gust of wind sends the padlock swinging wildly, screeching against the metal door. Fortune hopes the noise will cover her footsteps as she approaches; she wants the upper hand this time.

But as she reaches the entrance, a voice booms out at her.

"Ms Ngubu. Do come in."

Reflexively she withdraws her Luger. The man's voice echoes off the metal walls of the building, its Scottishness emphasised by the reverberations.

"You can pocket your weapon; you won't be needing it just now."

Fortune knows she'd kept out of sight of the door; she is no amateur. So how does he know it is her? How does he know she has a weapon? Did he see her getting out of the car? She moves to get a better position, her aim straight at the gap in the door. She does not like to be outmanoeuvred.

"I'd hoped you'd have more about you. Surely a hitman, or woman, doesn't hide."

Fortune bristles at the derision in his voice but resists the urge to step into the line of fire. Instead she says, "Who are you?"

The reply is a short harsh laugh, then, "I am Murdo Livan."

Fortune holds her Luger steady against the strengthening wind. "How do I know that's true? I don't know what you look like. I don't know anything about you."

A pause, then, "I emailed you. And you have my photo in your pocket."

Self-reproach warms Fortune's cheeks. *How did you not see this man last night? He was certainly watching you. Is it time you retired, girl?*

"Won't you come out, Mr Livan? Come into the sunshine so we can get to know each other."

After a moment's silence the shed door swings open fully.

Fortune glimpses a flash of something and strengthens her stance. The man steps out into the daylight. It takes her a moment to recognise the old smoker from the hotel, carrying a Barrett rifle if she isn't mistaken. The same type that she's brought with her, oiled and wrapped in her overnight bag.

"Relax," he smiles. "Take a seat." He nods towards Fortune's left. She risks a glance to the side and sees an old wooden bench. "We've got lots to talk about."

She stiffens. Against her better judgement she's walked into a trap. She thinks back to who might be wanting revenge on her but there are too many people to list, too many jobs to pick one out over another. *What you going to do, girl?* Despite the surety of her own shot, Fortune knows one bullet from that rifle at this short distance would be fatal. She sidesteps to the bench, holding her aim. As she lowers herself to the seat, the man lowers his rifle, somehow knowing Fortune's curiosity will hold her back from shooting. He takes his place next to her and rests back.

"What a beautiful day to be alive."

Fortune remains silent. Too many thoughts are racing through her head as she realises the weapon he carries is *her* rifle. There's the tell-tale scar on the barrel received from a job she'd done in Zurich twenty-two years ago. *Who is this man?* A shiver of danger runs through her. She knows, or knows of, virtually everyone in her tight-knit industry, but she can not place this man. How the hell does he know her?

"I see you are puzzled, perhaps even a little frightened." He smiles again as he indicates Fortune's rifle.

"Why have you brought me here, Mr Livan?" Fortune wants to know why she is going to die today.

"I was two months off getting married when you came to kill me. I might have had children, grandchildren even, if things had been different."

He tips his head back and Fortune notices for the first time the long narrow scar that runs down the side of his face, each end obscured by hairline and beard.

"You shot me once, then turned and walked away."

Fortune prides herself on her accuracy; there has never been a need to check that the job was done.

"I remember your face. Empty. Like you were shooting a rabbit." He shakes his head in remembrance, "But I survived. By the slimmest of chances, I lived. It took me years to recover." He turns angry eyes on her now. "I lost everything. My job, my fiancée, my future."

She remembers him now, he'd been a job for another client. She had known him as Ivan Dulmor then. She'd been in Switzerland anyway on another job and this had been a last minute booking. He is right – he was just another name on a list.

"So now you're going to kill me?"

Livan inclines his head in acknowledgement. "But before I do, I want you to tell me why you do it. Why do you choose to kill?"

She closes her eyes, lost in the memories of that day, the sun drying the bloodied dirt and the flies feasting on her father's brains. A child of five, woken by gunfire. Seeing her father dead on the ground, a man standing over her mother, seeing him shoot and walk away.

Fortune looks back at Livan. "I take one shot and walk away because that is what the killer did when he took the life of my mother and my father. When he took away my life."

It is a long time before Livan speaks. "So why choose murder to make your living?"

Fortune looks at him and shrugs. "It's all I've ever known. More men came and took me away, trained me to be a fighter, gave me the only skills I have."

Livan shakes his head, confused. His plan is to deal out retribution, not pity.

"For all these years hatred of you has eaten at my soul. Tracking you down has taken all my strength. But listening to that… that… suffering…' He stands and lays the rifle on the bench. "I'm heading back to the hotel. I might see you at the bar for a drink."

He turns away, picking his way through the thistles, turning briefly to look over his shoulder, raising his left hand in farewell. Fortune, too, lifts her left hand.

One shot.

He falls hard against the brick wall. She takes her time reaching him. This time she checks. *You've still got it, girl.*

THE LAST REPORT OF J.L WOODGATE

KELLY SCHWEIZER

"I remember when my mama used to tell me stories. We'd be straight out the bath, my little brother running through the cluster of rooms half dressed. He was always the naughty one. Not me though. I'd wait patiently by her chair while she tricked him into his clothes. Sometimes I'd giggle as she wrapped him up in her arms. Mama was silly back then.

Finally, she'd collapse into the rickety seat, her legs wrapped around my shoulders. When I climbed into her chair, I had to stretch my legs as long as they would go to touch the chair, perching carefully on the edge. Mama's legs didn't do that. They were always darker than mine too, with patches of purple and yellow at the front. When she sighed and sank back into the remains of the cushions, I knew it was story time and I would concentrate on the words tumbling from her lips. The screeching from the street faded and I even managed to ignore the way she yanked a comb through my hair. There was a magic in Mama's stories.

I don't think my brother knew that then or else I think my space in front of the chair wouldn't have been mine anymore. That's how I lost my best book too. He scrawled all over it in his silly crayons and the pictures weren't the same anymore. He didn't like it when I had something he didn't, even when Mama said we had to share. Luckily, he was far more interested in the other room. The big bed we all slept in was through there and Mama and I would watch him jumping on it through the beads in the door. He looked funny through them.

Mama never stopped telling me the story though and together we left the noisy flat behind.

No more thumping from upstairs or the tinny sounds from the bar below. No, Mama and me would go somewhere else, somewhere new. She told me of the fields, like the park but bigger, much bigger. The grass there was green and we could roll in it if we wanted to. Sometimes she'd tell me about the flowers that grew there, even taller than I am and I'm the tallest kid in our block. If I squeezed my eyes real tight, I could see the flowers. I'd try and imagine them again later that night, when we were supposed to be asleep. Through the beads, I could see Mama slumped in her chair. She would sit in the half light, her face screwed up like she was going to cry. I didn't like that. Instead, I would try and remember the other place from her stories but I couldn't do it without Mama. She's the one with the magic.

When we get there, do you think she can tell me about the fields again?"

I don't know why the kid looked at me. I was busy writing it down, writing it all down. I certainly didn't have any answers, not for her. What do you tell an eight-year-old looking for her mother? If she wasn't in this van with us, she was long gone. Maybe it would be kinder to tell her that now.

Still, my professor always said that we shouldn't guide our subjects too much so I kept my mouth shut. I waited for her to finish her story. I waited, my pen tapping impatiently, but all that happened was that those big brown eyes grew glassy and her lip began to wobble. Oh god, I hated it when kids cried. And why was she still looking at me? I was here for the stories, that was all. Everyone else in the van was staring at me expectantly so I offered her a reassuring smile.

"Sure, kid," I said, though even I didn't believe myself. "She'll tell you the story later."

Before she could ask me anything else, I turned back to my notes, adding to the story before I forgot anything. It was important to take good notes so that you could fill things out in the edits. Ideally, I should have recorded the whole thing but there hadn't been any time to grab my Dictaphone when the soldiers came. I had grabbed some clothes and the notebook by my mattress and joined the crowds. The only tools you need are a pen and some drive, they'd taught me once. I guess I would put that to the test now.

"When I was growing up," the old man began, "I dreamt of owning my own farm. A plot of land that was all mine. I'd grow some vegetables and keep a couple of animals. Some chickens, some pigs. Just enough to keep me busy. I'd come in from the fields and sit down for my dinner with my family. A wife. Two kids. A son and then a little girl, just like you. We'd share about our days over some good food that I picked myself.

That was my dream when I was your age. Other kids may have dreamt about being footballers or astronauts or doctors but all I wanted was some normalcy. Some independence. They were the things I thought adulthood could bring me.

An escape from the two rooms of our home and the lumpy mattress I shared with my three siblings. Someone had told me about a farm, you see. Or rather I had heard someone talking about it. The good old days, he had called them, as he swayed in his seat. I had to drag my father's body to the side to avoid him as he waved his pint around. He was telling everyone, whether they wanted to hear it or not, about his childhood on the family farm. I asked him why he left but I don't think he heard me over the crowds. Maybe he just didn't want to waste his time on a young boy.

Later that night, when my father snored loudly on the bed beside ours, I found myself remembering the wistful way he had talked about it. Remembering and fixating on it. Sometime in the night, as I tossed and turned, I decided that I would leave the city one day. I would leave it and would never look back until my feet carried me to a piece of land that would be all mine.

For years after that, I never gave up on my dream. Every penny that I managed to scrimp or steal, I stuck it in an old sock, one that was too threadbare to even try to fix. I kept it hidden under a loose floorboard in the kitchen, hardly daring to believe that with each coin I was one step closer to getting out."

The old man grew silent for a long time, staring absentmindedly at his knuckles. It was the young girl who finally prompted him to continue.

"Did you manage it? Did you have enough money?" she asked at last.

"No," he responded bitterly, "I never got enough money. One day I went to the floorboard and found it empty. My father was gloriously and obliviously drunk when he returned that night." He shook his head angrily.

"But I did get out of that house. I found a job, and then a wife, and then a teeny tiny shack of a cottage that was all ours. It was a mess but between us we cleaned it up. Painted it. Got some nice new curtains. It became a home after a while. More of one than I had ever known. And we were happy, happier still when my wife grew pregnant. We started growing some herbs and things out the back of the cottage, then some vegetables. We wanted chickens but the neighbours would have killed us. Her belly grew and grew as our garden was steadily filled with everything I could get my hands on. My boy, Jimmy, was born not long after. My wife loved that boy with everything she had. We both did. We poured everything we had into making that cottage a happy place, a home.

And it was.

For years after that. Jimmy grew and Lisa was born. Then Eddy. I grew carrots. Lettuces. Potatoes. Got an apple tree.

I would carry my produce proudly in to my wife. When I came home from work, she had transformed it into something wonderful.

I began to think I didn't need that old dream anymore. I had everything I needed right here in the city. It was enough. Even when the kids grew up and left home, we were happy. Our house was never empty. There were grandkids and spouses and friends always popping in. I felt my heart might just burst.

Then our Eddy came round with her youngest one with the nastiest cough I ever heard. I told her to get to the doctors but she said there were no appointments left. Too many people were sick so they were telling people to stay away. Rest up and have plenty of liquids. All this fuss for a bit of a cold, she scoffed as she fed the child on her knee from her plate. I should have pushed her on it but that wouldn't get you anywhere with our Eddy. Stubborn from the moment she took her first breath. Stubborn right until her last.

It didn't take long after that.

My garden withered to nothing as I neglected it. Instead, I soothed and bathed and offered what little comfort I could as my entire family coughed its way to the grave.

Within three months, all that was left was me and that apple tree in a barren city."

We were all silent after that. Nobody had any comfort to spare, not even for a frail and resigned old man who had shared his pain with us. We had all known too much pain to be surprised by it. All I could do was to keep writing as the words tumbled from him.

I watched as the young girl crossed to him wordlessly. She pulled herself into his lap and he held her to him.

"Maybe one day we'll find a farm with lots of fields. You, me and Mama," she offered.

He couldn't keep the resignation from his voice as he replied. "Maybe, kid. Maybe."

I couldn't focus on him for too long. The woman to my left was clutching at my arm in desperation. She was talking so quickly and in a language I couldn't recognise. I tried to tell her I didn't understand, I really did, but she didn't seem to notice. I've tried to copy it here – I might be able to find someone at the paper to translate it. Or at least I hope I can.

"Oh dieu, pourquoi je ne l'ai pas écoutée? Elle m'a dit de rester à la maison avec elle, mais j'étais tellement déterminé que j'avais raison. J'aurais pu me retourner à l'aéroport, mais j'étais tellement en colère contre elle que j'ai forcé un pied devant l'autre jusqu'à ce que je ne puisse pas rentrer chez moi si je le voulais. C'était juste un combat. Un petit bagarre idiot. Nous avions eu beaucoup au cours des années. Je l'aurais appelée le matin et m'excuserais. Je le savais même alors. Mais le téléphone de l'hôtel était mort. Mon mobile était mort. Tout le monde était mort.

Oh, dieu, laisse-la en sécurité, d'accord? Si je dois traiter dans un pays étrange avec des gens étranges, laissez-la sortir. De toutes les choses que je vous ai déjà demandées, c'est le plus important. S'il vous plaît, laissez-la être correcte, s'il vous plait."

Whatever she had been trying to tell us, it was lost as her words were claimed by her sobs. I tried to tune them out as I scribbled down the last of her story as best as I could. Maybe later, when I get to an office, someone can translate it for me. It might be worth something, maybe get me an award or two.

I looked up to see a young gentleman reach across to her. He carefully laid a hand on her shoulder and when she didn't shrug it off, he pulled her into an embrace. She leaned into it, crying until the stranger's shirt was soaked through with her tears. How I wished I had a camera with me. That was the shot to accompany this piece, I just knew it. I guessed we'd have to recreate it later. Get some actors… good ones, mind. I'd have to ask for some extra budget to do it but with a story like this, all the newspapers should be clamouring to hire me.

We sat in silence for a while, until the absence of sound grew too painful to bear. Eventually the young man who had comforted her returned to his own seat. He carefully wrapped his arms around himself, his eyes fixed on something none of us could see. When he spoke, I had to strain to listen to him.

"When I was getting ready to move here, they made us sit through a series of 'assimilation' workshops at uni. Hours and hours on the way language differs, the cultural changes, that kind of thing. I can remember sitting in the back of the hall and wondering why they were making us sit through this. It wasn't like I needed to learn a new language, or anything. I just wanted to come over and see what it was like in your classroom before I set up my own.

And then I got over here and everything is different. You drive on the wrong side of the road and don't know how to cross one. And don't even get me started on that stuff you call tea.

It was strange, but fine. Until I got sick. At home, I probably would have shaken it in a few days but I couldn't find the meds I usually use and I didn't fancy searching through a store for some. In fact, I didn't fancy leaving my bed at all.

I missed the first few days of it like that. I didn't even know that anything was wrong. Huh. Blissful ignorance, I guess. There were moments that I thought I might die and I was so absorbed in that painful thought that I barely even thought of the rest of this country. I was thinking of the home I didn't think I would ever see again. But I got better, and I began to hope that I would return there. I switched on my computer to book a flight and… nothing. Confused, I stumbled from my room to ask my neighbour if I could use theirs.

The smell in the corridor comes back to me whenever I close my eyes. Their bodies must have been lying there for days. I remember running from the building, hoping to find someone to help me.

It wasn't long before I realised that the world had died while fevers attacked my body. That I would die here too, so far from home…"

Editor's notes:

The writer stops here, the last few lines almost illegible. They were clearly in a hurry to finish their tale but were ultimately unable to. Considering the conditions that we found the notebook in, it is clear that this interruption was unplanned and unwelcome. The book itself was found stuffed between the workbench of a converted van and the metallic wall. Once perhaps it was used for cargo but the food scraps within suggest that it had been repurposed to transport people into the safe zone. It must have been one of the last vans to leave the city for it to have been used. We lost many vehicles as we tried to evacuate the survivors.

The team are still trying to piece together why exactly the van didn't make it to us. They followed the prescribed route perfectly and their escorts were among our most trained. We had made plans to accommodate them here at the compound. Many of them had useful skills we desperately needed. Those people should have made it past our walls but instead we're having to try and figure things out with the help of a tattered notebook, splattered with what I can only assume is the writer's blood. Some of the pages were stuck together when it landed on my desk. I've done my best to peel them apart careful but some parts were irretrievable. Considering this is one of the last surviving reports from those within the city, it is a tragedy that we cannot discover more.

Whoever these people were, it is the great loss of our compound that they were unable to join us. I'm sure they would have been invaluable to our research. We need all the help we can get these days.

TOMMY HARRIS
JOHN SIMMONDS

Wake up, son. Come on… come on…

I can't see anything!

Don't worry. I'm here now. Can you move?

Who are you? Oh, heavens…

Drink this. Slowly, slowly. Don't worry, lad. What's your name?

What's wrong with my eyes? Oh god, my legs hurt.

What's your name, Private?

Harris, Tommy Harris.

Listen lad, you're in a shell hole. You've been hit. Try to take a few deep breaths.

My face feels like it's on fire.

Slowly now, Harris… take another sip… well done… I'm Sergeant Simpson.

What's happening, Sarge?

You've been hit in the leg and face. I'll wipe the blood a bit…

Heck, that hurts.

Harris, listen to me. I need you to concentrate. I need you sitting up… here you go…

Ohhhhh…

Don't faint on me now. Deep breaths. Here, let's get those eyes clear…

I still can't see.

You've copped it badly. Here, let's get you straighter.

My legs…

I'm going to put a tourniquet on your left leg. Don't want you bleeding anymore.

Aghhhh – crikey, that's tight, Sarge…

Rest your head back, Harris. Tommy, you say?

Yes, Sarge. Tommy Harris. Second West Yorkshires.

Yorkshire lad, eh? Do you remember what happened?

We went over the top. I remember a bang… well… then you turned up, Sarge, that's all.

You're safe now.

Bloomin' heck, I'm right groggy, Sarge.

You've taken some shrapnel in the face, Tommy. I can't take it out at the moment.

Am I going to die? I'm only nineteen…

You're not going to die, lad, not if I can help it.

Are my eyes going to be okay?

They're pretty messed up, I'm afraid. Let's worry about that after we get you back behind our lines.

I'm feeling really rum, Sarge… like I'm going to faint.

Tommy, you've got to stay with me now. As soon as it's clear up there, I'll get you out.

Don't leave me here, will you…?

Not on your nelly. Listen up – I think the shelling has stopping.

My bloomin' ears are ringing, Sarge. How much of a mess am I in, really?

Your left leg's been smashed up badly, but I think you'll be able to walk with a bit of luck.

I play football back home. This flippin' war…

Well, I reckon your chances of playing for England might have gone for a while, Tommy.

I'm a Leeds supporter.

Leeds? Well, lad, if you'd told me that, I wouldn't have jumped in this shell hole!

What about you, Sarge?

I'm a Birmingham City man myself. That chap you've got playing up front is a jewel, Tommy.

Great manager as well, Sarge. Herbert Chapman. I reckon next year… oh, that hurts!

Right, lad. The hun seem to have stopped shelling. There's been nothing for a few minutes now.

Sarge, don't leave me now, will you…?

Tommy, I told you I wouldn't and I'm not going to. We need to wait here just a while longer.

I won't be able to walk, Sarge. I just know it.

Once I've got you out of this shell hole, I can carry you on my back.

Okay, Sarge. Thanks, Sarge.

Right. Let's go. It's quiet, so we should try to move now.

Won't they see us?

No chance, there's so much smoke and fog about, I'll be lucky not to land us both back into another hole!

Okay, Sarge. Tell me what you want me to do.

Right, here you go. Put your hands around my neck…

Owww! Stop a minute… ow!

Hmphhhh – this isn't going to work. I can't get any leverage. I'll climb out, and pull you up after.

Where are you, Sarge?

Quiet, quiet, don't want the entire world knowing where Tommy Harris is, do we?

Is that your hand, Sarge?

Yes, Tommy. Give me your other one…

Ohhhhh…

Quiet, lad! Bite your lip. Right… one more pull… uhhhh. There you go. We're out.

What can you see, Sarge?

There's no one about. I hope there's no gas. Hang on a minute while I get my breath.

Sarge?

Yes, Tommy?

If I die, there's a note in my pocket. It's for my mum. Can you…?

Of course. What's her name?

Dinah. She'd be heartbroken. There's only me left for her.

What about your dad?

He's gone. Died working in the pits a few years back.

Don't worry, son. You can give her the note yourself. What was your dad's name?

Eric.

Right, Tommy Harris, only son of Eric and Dinah – I'm going to lift you up on my back and get us both moving.

Righto, Sarge. Sarge?

Yes, lad?

Thanks.

You'd do the same for me, Tommy.

I haven't got my rifle, Sarge.

Not to worry. His Majesty's Army has another one waiting for you.

Do you know which way you're going, Sarge?

Course I do. Away from the smell of those rotten huns.

Uhhhhhh – Sarge! Sarge? Are you okay?

I slipped. It's bloody tricky walking through this mud with you on my back. Hang on, I'll…

What's that? What happened?

Stuck my foot in a hole. Bloody hell, my knee's gone. Bloody hell!

Sarge? Sarge, are you okay?

I've twisted my knee, Tommy. Keep your head down.

Sarge, what are we going to do?

I don't know, lad.

I can try to help, Sarge. If we take it slowly…

We'll have to crawl. Keep a good hold of my hand. Don't want you getting lost.

I wouldn't know where to go, Sarge.

I do. We'll be fine.

What if they start bombing again?

Let's hope they don't – and if they do, let's hope their aim's as bad as their breath – bloody huns.

I can't do it, Sarge. I can't push myself enough.

Come on, Private. Show me how strong you Leeds boys are.

Hrrrrrr – it's no good, Sarge. I can't.

Well, we can't stay here. This smoke is going to blow away soon and…

What, Sarge? What then?

We'd be done for, lad. Best bet is to get you back to the shell hole, I reckon.

Where is it?

Behind us, Tommy. We only managed a few steps. I think I can push myself – hold on to me.

I'm scared, Sarge.

Hold on, lad! Hang on to my… ooooffff.

Sarge, where are you?

I'm in the bloomin' shell hole. Crawl towards my voice. And keep your head down.

Oww… sorry, Sarge!

Not to worry. At least you're back in. But please, can you get your scrawny backside off my face?

Sorry, Sarge. Sarge?

Yes, lad.

What do we do now?

We'll wait here and hope that our boys find us first.

Is it still foggy up there?

Most of the smoke has cleared now. We'll be out of sight down here.

Sarge, have you got any morphine?

No. Sorry, lad.

It's okay. I'll manage. Have you got any cigarettes, Sarge? I could do with a puff.

Here you go. Hang on, I've got some matches somewhere.

What if the huns find us first?

They're not all animals. Most of them are ordinary blokes like you and me.

What do you do, Sarge? You know, when you're not in a shell hole on the Somme?

I'm a butcher. Got a shop in Sparkhill back in Brum.

Are you married?

Yes. My wife's Enid. Two boys, Barry and Tim.

How old?

Barry's five, Tim's three.

Do you miss them?

Of course I do. Been married ten years now. My old man was a butcher too.

Is he still around?

Lost him ten years back. Still got my old mum, though. Want another ciggy?

Thanks, Sarge. Shouldn't really because my mum's always telling me how bad they are for you.

Ha – very funny, lad. I doubt it's the fags'll kill you! What did you do before, Tommy? Before this all kicked off.

I'm apprenticing, Sarge. Plastering. I've done a bit of painting and decorating as well. Working for my uncle.

Keeping it in the family then.

Not anymore, Sarge. Not sure how I'm going to paint anything much if I can't see.

Don't give up yet, Tommy. Your right eye's gone, but the other one might be okay with a bit of luck.

This whole thing is messed up, Sarge. I don't even know why we're fighting.

Not our job to question why, Private. We do what we're told. Follow orders and hope for the best.

Never get any of those generals on the front line, do we, Sarge?

Steady on, lad. Don't want to hear any talk like that.

Sorry, Sarge.

Quiet now, I think there's someone coming. Put that ciggy out.

Shall we give them a holler?

No – could be our boys, but I can't be sure one way or the other.

Do the Germans take prisoners?

Like I said, they're doing their job, like you and me. Shhhhh…

Have they gone?

I'll take a look. I'll need you to push me up a little – I can't see from here. There you g…

Sarge! Bloody hell, Sarge. Did you cop it? Sarge – talk to me, talk to me. Sarge? Who's there? Who's there…? Please – I can't see… I'm Tommy Harris, second West Yorkshires.

THE ROSES & THE WEEDS
ELINORA WESTFALL

Ollie talks.

Not that Bridget listens. She's too absorbed in the mundane task of fastening her bra, a simple action frustrated by a twinge of back pain, a lingering stiffness in her shoulder, and her own condemning thoughts: *You're getting too old to shag in a van.*

Apparently, she's not getting too old for Ollie, though, because he keeps coming back for more; she's continually mystified, flattered, and unable to resist. He's too beautiful. He is too close to physical perfection.

Despite this however, her interactions with him frequently disappoint, her sexual and aesthetic experience diminishes substantially with the inevitable occurrence of one very simple thing: He speaks.

She wishes that she had kept a written record of all the epic bloody nonsense that has come out of his mouth over the years because she could have gained some kind of minor social media fame and parleyed a book deal out of it to boot: *Shit My Stupid Shag Buddy Says.* It occurs to her that as far as sordid shag buddies go, she has run the gamut from an Oxford graduate to this, the man who thought that when his sister was pregnant with twins, she'd be pregnant for eighteen months rather than nine. It's her typical anti-accomplishment: From the gutter to the stars and back again.

As Ollie blathers about football, he leans over to tie his trainers and this singular movement initiates a glorious symphony of muscle and flesh in stirring, magnificent counterpoint with one another. She longs to trace the perfect trapezoid muscles within reach but doesn't, knowing that he would interpret this as an overture for a second go-round, which she's not really up for because of the pulled muscle in her lower back and various other reasons that she won't let herself think about.

So, she lets him go on and on about Liverpool and the proliferation of their bloody stupid fans up North.

"They're everywhere," he says, "everywhere! I don't get it. I mean, there must be a Brazilian of them here."

Bridget successfully resists the urge to bang her head on the side of the van.

"Don't you think?" He gazes up at her.

Aw, bless, he's trying to engage her in conversation; it would be touching if it weren't so pathetic. "A Brazilian," she says flatly. She rubs her aching shoulder and pulls on the hideous yellow work apron; she has to give the café credit for picking the one colour that makes all pasty white people look like utter shite.

"Yeah. You know. Like a lot. Like more than a million?" Ollie rolls his eyes. "Know maths is not your strong suit, Bridget, but, Jesus, everyone knows that."

"It's billion," Bridget enunciates with a certain sarcastic slowness that immediately reminds her of Vita, and that makes her want to slam her head against the van until she is unconscious. "You mean billion. Not Brazilian."

He's sceptical. "You sure?"

"A Brazilian is a person. From Brazil." She forces out the point between clenched teeth. "The country."

The light-bulb goes off over Ollie's handsome head, offering only a bare minimal illumination of knowledge.

"Oh. Right, right," he nods vigorously, "okay. Yeah. That makes sense." Slow, graceful, and lazy, he pulls on his shirt. "We doing this again next week, maybe?"

"Maybe," she lies, and ties the apron at her back with stiff fingers, catching a hangnail on the waistline of her jeans; she wore jeans to work today and amazingly Claud didn't call her out on it. Ollie said it was because she looked stunning in them. He rarely compliments her, so she figures it must be true. Again, she thinks of Vita, who once said – *you should always wear jeans, it ought to be the law of the land* – woozily stated after one nap, two orgasms and three glasses of wine, so she was feeling uncharacteristically munificent that day. And again, she wishes she would stop thinking of Vita, at least immediately after shagging idiots.

Ollie laughs. "It's weird. You're really like a bloke

sometimes." He pulls a face. "Shit, that sounds really gay, doesn't it?"

She stares at the abandoned used condom on the floor of the van – flaccid, sad, and inanimate as if it were the eviscerated hydro-skeleton of some strange jellyfish.

"Yeah. It does." She grabs her jacket, pushes at the van's heavy door with her good shoulder, and she's free. For the moment, anyway.

•

At home, the windows are fogged up with steam from the beef stew she's reheating on the Aga. She's staring at her own reflection, sullied and blurry, hair all over the bloody place, curling about her jaw, slipping out from her poor excuse for a ponytail. An unremarkable colour at the best of times, but in this steam bleached reflection it is even more limp, even more of a non-colour – an insipid pale brown with a fleck of early grey. And her eyes, staring back at her like the eyes of a ghost, almost too pale to see, almost the same colour as the sky.

"What's this?" her dad pipes up. He's fishing for something in the drawer of the kitchen dresser.

She turns around. "What's what?"

He's holding a champagne cork. "Taittinger's? When were you drinking Taittinger's?" He laughs, his eyes twinkle.

Oh, you – stupid slapper, stroppy trailer trash, foul-mouthed slattern. Who do you think you are? Someone worthy of fine champagne?

It's not the kind voice of her father, but the voice of the past that fills her head so unexpectedly.

It's been said that the past is another country; in Bridget's case, it is more than that. It is an enemy combatant. Any object that could possibly function as a passport into this hostile territory runs the risk of emotional high treason and as such is mercilessly discarded. When she turned thirty (nine whole years ago…) she trashed or burned nearly everything sentimental. Including herself. But there were clothes, photos, keepsakes, a napkin with a heart drawn on it from a first official date, all consigned to the flames or the rubbish heap. The cork is an emissary from a different part of the past, however, and she should have got rid of it but couldn't. Not yet, anyway. The cork, the same one she absently touched to her lips that night as she stood in Room 503 of the Belgravia Hotel, fully clothed and ready to leave but unable to as she helplessly stared down at Vita, sprawled face down on the bed in a dead sleep.

Oh, you…

Bridget jams a wooden spoon into the dense, beefy glop of stew, which plops ominously like a volcano stirring from a dormancy of a thousand years.

"Don't remember when."

"Looks recent." He turns the cork over in his hand.

"Bloody cork expert now, are you?" She throws him a sideways glance through the steam and he smiles at her, that sweet smile that always gets her right in the chest. You'd better not ever bloody die, she thinks. A thought so often passing through her head that it had now become a sort of mantra, something she had to think daily to save his life.

He gives a vague nod of his head, amusement behind his eyes as he places the cork carefully back into the drawer.

The front door opens, the hall floorboards creak, and for the briefest of moments she feels the gritty unevenness of those floorboards against her bloody cheek, and hears that voice in her head: *God, it was fun breaking you, Bridget.*

"Granddad," Ryan drops a school bag down by the leg of the dining table and claps a hand over his granddad's shoulder.

"What's for dinner?"

She feels his presence behind her. She wants to turn and hug him, draw him close and apologise for everything: for the stew, for the bad weather, for not knowing who his father was… for being such a disappointment.

"Thought you ate at school?" she says instead.

She hears him groan, can just about make out his reflection behind her in the window.

"Bloody salad."

He wraps his arms around her waistline and she swats at his wrists with her free hand.

"Language."

Her dad hums sympathetically from the corner of the room.

"What's new?" she asks absently, glancing at him before turning to the washing up in the sink.

"The usual," he shrugs. He's wearing the hoody she bought him for Christmas.

"Sounds fascinating," she says, mouth full affectionate sarcasm as she notices the holes in his cuffs.

"Actually, there is a bit of news, about our hermit next-door neighbour."

She feels the skin just above the veins in her wrist begin to buzz and she plunges her hands into the too-hot water.

"Vita?" She doesn't know why she's asking, they only have one neighbour for miles around.

"So, what's the news?" she prompts while Ryan nods through a gulp of Coke from a bottle she hadn't noticed he was holding.

"Looks like she's got herself a girlfriend."

Bridget is glad she's facing the window. She waits for the sky and the land to do their usual trick of calming her, bringing her peace. She studies the thin band of clouds frosting the blue sky, the way the wind presses into the long, faded grass. She squeezes the steel wool pad in her hand. Watery brown gunk from the pot she's been scrubbing surrenders to the drain and she predicts by the end of the week she'll have to take apart the pipes again to work out the clog. Didn't expect her to remain on the market forever, did you? Despite the fact that she was a middle-aged woman… *a widow, a posh bitch, a recluse…*

Put like that, Bridget asks herself, *why are you so keen on her, you dozy cow?*

She dries her hands with a towel and turns around. Keeping her hands busy always settles her nerves. She can tell by the way Ryan looks at her that he's waiting for her to trot out some smart-arsed remark, some homophobic put-down.

"Good," she says softly. She clears her throat and tries it again – this time firmer and louder, and almost convinces herself. "That's good."

"You met her?" her dad asks from the dresser. He's left the drawer open. She stares at it, unblinking, while Ryan answers.

"Briefly. She was leaving when we showed up. They were kind of giggly together. It was cute."

Bridget twirls the limp, damp dish-towel into a sinewy rope and attempts fashioning a hangman's noose out of it.

"She seems cool. Didn't talk to her for long but she was funny, smart. Her name is Sacha. Works in finance or something. There was an article on her and her family in the Courier yesterday – Clarissa was telling me. God, I think even Clarissa likes her – anyway, the family's really posh and they set up some new scholarship fund for, you know, 'underprivileged students'." Ryan employs the good old air quotes around the phrase – an Elizabeth sarcasm speciality, and again Bridget suspects that he has a crush on Vita, even as she simultaneously acknowledges the fierce irrationality of her ridiculous jealousy. At this pathetic moment, she is even jealous of the Jeep Cherokee she sees parked in Vita's drive every morning, jealous of it for its close proximity to its owner, not to mention the front seat.

Oh, Christ, you are bananas.

"Maybe you should apply," her dad says.

"I'm not underprivileged. Right, Mum?"

Bridget hums absently.

"Mum?"

"Yeah?"

Amused, Ryan smirks. "Why are you making a noose with the dish-towel?"

Her dad propels himself from the edge of the dresser. "My cue to leave, before she gets any ideas."

Oh, that joke isn't funny anymore.

"I'll join you." Ryan follows his granddad from the room.

Bridget hears the creak of the sofa as they sit down in the sitting room, a pause, then the welcome murmur of the television.

She fishes for her phone in the pocket of her jeans, flicks the screen on and hits Google.

This is what she has become… someone who stalks a former shag buddy with whom you have the grave and stupid misfortune of being in love. It's exhausting. She yawns. After a good ten minutes, she is finally online and hopping to the Courier's website, where the fluff piece on Vita's new woman is found easily enough.

In Bridget's mind, there are two types of English woman: The Roses and the Weeds. Vita, of course, is a Rose: pale and elegant, seemingly perfect, secretly thorny, and bitchily unrepentant when blood is drawn. She herself is, of course, a sturdy English Weed: tough, available, and usually trampled upon by blokes in obsessive pursuit of the Roses. Ollie alone is proof of the paradox. When they weren't shagging, they were drinking and talking about Vita; a shared loathing of the same woman bonded them more than sex ever did.

But Jennifer Elena Sacheverell Easley Parmenter – Jesus Christ, Bridget thinks, what kind of person needs five fucking names? – is a voluptuous variation on the Weed: a bit horsey-looking but well-groomed, well-dressed, and possessing abundant dark locks a la Nigella Lawson. Not to mention big tits. No, she is not a common English Weed, this lady's not for trampling. She's the weed that will wrap with luxurious abandon around everything in a garden till it's hers, that will scale the stone walls of the mansion until her wild garlands smother everything in sight. In the photo, she's smiling handsomely, about ready to burst out of her blouse, and sandwiched between two happy teenagers and a man, whom Bridget is pretty certain she might have shagged.

Bridget reads on. Jennifer is a CEO of a digital music company. Even though she and her fucking ex-husband, a fucking barrister, both went to fucking Cambridge she fucking supported her fucking son when he wanted to go to fucking Oxford. Her fucking father is a fucking marquis and – here Bridget dies a little – her fucking Italian mother is a fucking 'member of the distinguished, aristocratic Milanese family' that includes the filmmaker Luchino Fucking Visconti.

Defeated, she leans back in the chair. Sure, great. That's

just great. She manages one final, rallying thought: Can Jennifer single-handedly replace a toilet? Plumb in a washing machine or rewire a house? Bet not. Top that, bitch. "Fucking slag."

Bridget does not realise she's said this aloud until Ryan calls loudly from the couch, "Who's a fucking slag?"

"The Queen," she shouts back.

"Too right. Always thought she was a bit tarty with all those hats."

She scowls, realises her mother was right so many years ago when she still had possession of at least a few marbles: Someday you'll have one of your own, and they'll be mouthing off to you the way you do to me, and you'll be sorry then.

She is very sorry indeed. About a lot of things, but not that.

IT IS YOUR BIRTHDAY

JOE WILLIAMS

You are thirty years old today. People have been telling you that this is a big birthday, but you don't think it is. It is the same as any other birthday, except that the number is divisible by ten, and there is nothing particularly special about that.

There have been ten thousand nine hundred and fifty-seven days since you were born. You worked this out last week when Pat at work told you that thirty is a big birthday. If people counted their ages in days then most people would not think the ten thousand nine hundred and fifty-seventh day was very important. Ten thousand nine hundred and fifty-seven is not divisible by ten. It is not divisible by anything other than one and itself, because it is a prime number, which makes it a much more interesting number than thirty, but most people would not realise this.

When you wake up at eight thirteen in the morning you don't even remember that it is your birthday at first.

The only thing different to usual is that you do not have to go to work. You have not been to work for the last three days, so this does not feel unusual. You have taken the week off, because you know that if you were at work then your colleagues would put balloons on your desk, and give you an oversized card signed by everyone in the office, and you would be expected to bring a cake. You don't like people to make a fuss about your birthday, and you don't particularly like cake, which is why you have taken the week off work.

You are reminded that it is your birthday when you log into Facebook. Forty-eight people have posted on your wall. They have written messages like 'Happy birthday mate', 'Many happy returns' and 'Wow, the big 3-0!'. You have also received an email from your friend Barney, who works in computer security and doesn't use social media because he is concerned about privacy and protecting his personal information. Barney lives in San Francisco but never forgets your birthday. He sent the email at five twenty-three this morning, which would have been nine twenty-three on the previous evening in San Francisco. At this time of year, San Francisco uses Pacific Daylight Time, which is eight hours behind British Standard Time. He would have known that this meant that you would receive his email when you woke up this morning.

You spend the rest of the morning reading a book about the composer Richard Strauss. You drink two cups of coffee. At two eleven in the afternoon, you see your parents pull up outside your house in their car. They are eleven minutes later than they said they would be, but this does not surprise you because they are always late. They have brought a birthday card and presents wrapped in paper with pictures of champagne bottles and glasses. You unwrap the presents and find that they are a pair of Levi 501 jeans, a pale brown shirt from Marks & Spencer, and a boxed set of bottled ales brewed by Marstons.

You have arranged to go out for a late lunch at The Silver Fox. The Silver Fox is a gastropub. Your Dad drives you all in your parents' car, and you arrive at two fifty-six. The pub is not very busy because it is a Tuesday afternoon and the lunchtime rush is over. For a starter you eat lamb koftas, and for your main course you have chicken and leek pie. You decide not to have a dessert but your parents both do. All of you agree that the food is excellent. You share a bottle of Pinot Grigio white wine with your Mum, and after the meal your Dad insists that you should drink whisky to celebrate your big birthday, so you both have a glass of Lagavulin. He says this is the only drink he is having because he is driving, so he might as well make it a good one. He says you are only thirty once, which is obvious. Your parents pay the bill, which comes to ninety-seven pounds and ten pence, but they add a tip to make a total of one hundred and ten pounds. That is a tip of approximately eleven point three percent, which you consider to be quite generous, but fair because both the food and the service were excellent.

After the meal you all go to The Clayton Arms. The Clayton Arms is a pub but not a gastropub. You arrive there at five forty-six and meet Rob. Rob is your brother. He has just finished work and is dressed in a white shirt and smart black trousers. Rob works for a company who sell and repair vending machines. He buys drinks for you and your parents. He has already bought one for himself. Your Dad has a pint of lager, even though he is driving. Your Mum says that he shouldn't have had another drink, but he says it will be fine.

Rob is twenty-eight but has already made a list of things to do before he is thirty. He has done very few of the things on his list, and only the easy ones, like going to a music festival, and drinking a pint of every guest ale in The Clayton Arms in a single evening. He has yet to run a marathon or visit Thailand. Some of the items on his list are preposterous. You think it is very unlikely that he will see the Earth from space in the next two years, and you would be very surprised if he had sex with any member of Little Mix, never mind all four of them at the same time. Rob once told you that you should also make a list of things to do before you are thirty, but you didn't want to, and now it is too late. You tell him you have made a list of things to do before you are thirty-one, and that there is only one thing on the list, which is to be thirty, which you have now done. He doesn't think this is as funny as you do.

When your parents have finished their drinks, they say they are going home. Your Mum pulls your hand under the table and pushes forty pounds cash into it, then they leave. You and Rob each have another pint of lager, and after that you go to Wetherspoons, where you have arranged to meet Louisa. Louisa is Rob's girlfriend. They have been together for almost three years, with two short breaks. You arrive at Wetherspoons at seven forty-one. It is busy, even though it is a Tuesday night. Louisa is not there yet, so you buy two more pints of lager.

Louisa arrives a few minutes later, with her friend Amy, who you have never met. They both wish you a happy birthday. Amy works at the Department for Work and Pensions as a Statistical Officer. You ask if she knows your friend Stefan, who also works at the Department for Work and Pensions, and she says that she does. When she finds out that you are thirty years old, she says she doesn't understand why people think it is a big birthday just because it is divisible by ten. When you mention that it is also ten thousand nine hundred and fifty-seven days, she remarks that at least that is a prime number.

You leave Wetherspoons at ten fourteen because you have been out for almost the whole afternoon and you are tired. Rob, Louisa and Amy stay for another drink. They all wish you happy birthday again, and Amy says it was nice to meet you.

When you get home, you make toast, drink one of the Marstons brewery ales which your parents gave you, and play online poker. In the online poker room, no one knows it is your birthday. You are a good poker player, but you should not play when you have been drinking. You make too many mistakes. You stop playing at one forty-six in the morning because you are now very tired.

It is no longer your birthday. Despite your mistakes, you are exactly seven pounds in profit.

Before you go to bed, you check Facebook. You have twenty-six more birthday messages on your wall, including one from your cousin Sonia which is a picture of a very large cake, and a friend request from Amy, which you accept.

To find out more about the Crossing The Tees Book Festival, visit our website…

www.crossingthetees.org